BRODIE McHAGGIS

BRODIE McHAGGIS

AND THE SECRET OF LOCH NESS

Helen Campbell

Chloe Publishing

First published in Great Britain in 2005
by Chloe Publishing Ltd, PO Box 4, Halkirk, Caithness, KW12 6XL, Scotland

A CIP catalogue record of this book is available from the British Library

ISBN 0-9551386-0-4
ISBN 978-0-9551386-0-7

Printed, typeset and bound in Great Britain by
Highland Printers, Inverness, Scotland

Second Edition 2006

www.hcampbell.com
www.chloepublishing.com
www.brodiemchaggis.com

With love and thanks

Donald, for your patience and encouragement

Mum, for always being there

Carna, for that special phone call

History, Legend or Myth …

will you ever really know …?

PROLOGUE

The Haggis

The haggis is an odd-looking creature. Newly born haggises, or haggisen, could be mistaken for ginger-red cotton wool balls running around on three matchsticks. Their ability to run and swim with only three legs, and use their feet as hands and fingers too, is both comical and astounding. They love to sing and their bagpipe-like wails can be heard for miles around. Seeing the haggis at work and at play is both an incredible and inspiring sight to watch.

They live in and around the heather-clad hillside of Dunroamin, preferring open spaces to forests, although they believe that the rowan tree is key to their survival. They have strong superstitions about kelpies and witches and believe people to be a wild myth from centuries ago.

Only one, fearless haggis has the unusual hunger for delving into the unknown …

he said nodding towards the water. 'You have to believe me when I say that there is a kelpie living in Darmaeddie Loch. I know we have never seen it, but it's there. That's why you can't swim in the loch.'

Brodie frowned at his father and looked back to the loch.

Jock stood on all three of his legs and tripled back and forth along the shore as he spoke to Brodie. 'Now, this story you seem to have in that wee mind of yours about the people of the Highlands is simply … simply myth - it's pure and utter haggiswallop. There are no such things as people and the Highlands don't exist. Trust me, I know what I'm talking about.'

Brodie twitched his long, fluted nose and the corners of his mouth curled in frustration as he muttered under his breath. He looked down at the pebble he was rolling around in his eight toe-like fingers before looking back out to the loch. The slight breeze rippled the surface and the water glistened under the sun like a million fireflies were dancing upon it. He shook his head and looked back to his father who was now sitting down in the heather trying to blow a yellow butterfly off the end of his nose. His round eyes crossed as he watched the butterfly cleaning the pollen from its feet.

'But Dad, the stories must've come from somewhere - don't you think? How … why …? I mean … oh what's the use,' he grumped, stamping his foot in frustration. It was clear that his father, or anyone else for that matter, didn't believe in those bare skinned animals - people. 'So, why then if we haven't seen a kelpie or people do we believe that just the kelpie exists?' Brodie paused briefly and flicked his eyes up at the swarm of midges still hovering above him. 'I just don't understand, Dad.'

The midges took one look at the challenging glint in Brodie's eyes and scarpered. A satisfied grin formed around Brodie's mouth.

Jock was becoming dizzy at trying to blow the butterfly off his nose and he sighed irritably. 'Questions, questions, questions - when will they ever end? Son - kelpies are dangerous and will entice you into the water. Just look out there and put some thought into it. How many rowan trees do you see?'

Brodie flinched at his father's sharp tone and surveyed the loch thoughtfully. He was right - there were no trees out there. But that didn't explain why nobody had ever seen a kelpie. Brodie was about to ask another question when a familiar, ringing voice interrupted him.

'Jock McHaggis … Jock Mc …'

Jock swung around to see Angus's tousled body tumbling from the McMail burrow at high speed. 'Yes, yes Angus. Slow down and catch your breath.' He sighed with impatience as he waited for Angus to deliver the message. 'So, where's the fire?'

Angus mopped the sweat from his ginger-red brow, hurriedly brushed the peat from his fur and looked at Jock quizzically as he untwisted his three legs from each other. He glanced around himself. 'Er … fire …?'

'Well if there's no fire, what's the rush then?' snapped Jock. His cool eyes penetrated Angus as he tried to suck whatever message he was supposed to deliver from him as quickly as possible. Jock McHaggis was a very impatient haggis and always frightened poor Angus.

Angus's tongue suddenly felt like it didn't belong to him. It flapped around uncontrollably as he stuttered and stammered his way through the message he'd been instructed to deliver.

'Y-y-you're banted wack at D-D-D-rumdrui.'

'You mean I'm wanted back at Drumdrui,' said Jock impatiently rolling his eyes. 'What for?' The sharp delivery of words seemed to hit Angus like a stone between the eyes. He backed off slightly and composed himself before replying, his eyes focused on Jock's three feet.

'Uhm … they didn't say, sir. Just said that I fould shind you - and Brodie,' he said shooting Brodie a nervous glance, 'as poon as sossible.'

Brodie sniggered.

Jock fumed. 'Well you've found me! Who're they? Oh, never mind. Tell them I'm on my way.'

Feeling relieved, Angus nodded hurriedly and zipped back into the burrow on his way to find the McNorrens and the McNeils. He had to hurry so that he could get back before Jock to make sure he didn't miss anything. This was the most exciting message he'd delivered in a long while. Everyone had been summoned back to Drumdrui, but he didn't know why.

Angus McMail spent his days whizzing around the Dunroamin hillside, delivering messages to the haggis community through his network of high-speed burrows buried deep within the peaty soil. It didn't have to be an emergency to make him run fast. He knew of no other speed - stop, or go like the fur on his bottom was on fire.

No other haggis was allowed in his network of burrows. So according to Angus, nothing should be ahead as he sped along the burrow, listening carefully for the echo coming back. On occasion, he had slammed into a pile of earth left by a rabbit burrowing through and had lain concussed for a few hours. The duller the echo that came back was a warning that there could be trouble ahead. The echoes were good today and Angus just kept on running.

The butterfly seemed too content to move on, so Jock finally brushed it off his nose with his finger, trying not to damage its delicate frame. 'Come on Brodie, it's obviously important,' said Jock sternly and he galloped up the hillside away from the loch, pleased of the interruption from Brodie's questions.

Brodie looked at the position of the sun in the sky and the

shadows cast on the ground by the trees. It was nearing teatime. Fuming silently, he took his anger out on the pebble and threw it into the air a few times before launching it into the water. 'What could be any more important than knowing what's out there?' He sighed dolefully before reluctantly turning on his leathery feet to go home.

Brodie did not see the pebble shoot back out of the water and land on the shore as he obediently sped through the heather after his father.

CHAPTER TWO

A Missing Haggis

Brodie stood at the top of the hill and looked down the valley at the stream of ginger-red fur as haggises bustled from their burrows and gathered within the circle of rowan trees in Drumdrui. Their panicked tones filtered up the hillside like an army of inflating and deflating bagpipes.

'What's up Dad?' he said, staring questioningly down at the commotion.

Jock narrowed his eyes with concern. 'I don't know, but I think we're about to find out.' Without another word, Jock bounded down the valley and into the centre of the thickening crowd of haggises. He quickly scanned the hundreds of worried-looking faces until his crystal-blue eyes rested on Mirg McVey.

Mirg, a very old and greying haggis, hobbled through the crowd towards him. He had injured a leg many years before when he fell out of a rowan tree, trying, without much success, to prove his theory that haggises could climb trees. He looked slightly anxious as he acknowledged Jock.

'Thank goodness you've arrived. The tension is building up here pretty bad.'

'I seem to have missed something,' said Jock feeling frustrated and hoping that somebody would explain to him what was going on.

'Sorry, I thought you knew,' said Mirg, flicking at the greying fur around his chin with his eight toe-fingered hand - or maybe it was his foot. At sixty-one years old, he was among one of the oldest haggises around and had been leader of the Haggis Community Council for longer than anyone could remember. His misty-grey eyes, which had lost their youthful crystal-blue glow, darted from left to right as he watched the swell of alarmed haggises form in front of him.

'Iron McGillis has gone missing - been gone since early this morning,' he said through a hurried whisper. 'His mother swears he's been taken by the evil forces - says he has been known to stray outside the bounds of the Silent Protector. Thinks he may have been dragged into the loch by a kelpie. She and that … husband of hers are stirring things up again. We've got a lot of smoothing of ruffled fur to do, Jock.'

Jock darted his eyes towards Brodie. 'Go to The Bothy,' he instructed.

Brodie knew better than to argue with his father at a time like this and he nosed his way through the thick crowd of haggis fur towards the entrance burrow to The Bothy.

'What if he's tried swimming in the loch? Every haggis knows not to swim in there - what with a resident kelpie,' said Jock through a hissed whisper.

'Yes … the illusive kelpie that none has witnessed,' said Mirg, wistfully nodding his oval-shaped head. 'Hard for youngsters to be afraid of something they haven't seen. I've never known anyone to swim in that loch. However, we are talking about Iron McGillis here,' he said as he turned and made his way to the centre of Drumdrui. 'He's a law unto himself.'

Jock's four nostrils turned red and flared with rage. 'We should get him - and his parents - to eat a few cockroaches in public.' A faint smile played around his determined mouth. 'That'll get him to behave himself!'

Mirg sighed patiently. 'Tut, tut, Jock. We will do nothing of the sorts. Firstly, we must get him back here safely ... if nothing's happened to him already.'

'And if he has stepped outside of the Silent Protector, how do you propose we do that? Are we supposed to follow him? And, if the kelpie has got him, he's lost forever,' said Jock, beginning to sound worried.

'Hmmm … yes, you're probably right. Come on - we'll need to address the community.' Mirg muttered continuously to himself as he threaded his way through the maze of panicked haggises. He hobbled up onto a lichen-covered stone that was overhung by a large, very leafy, rowan tree. Jock followed him and scanned the hundreds of worried-looking haggis eyes. He lowered his oval frame and sat beside Mirg with two of his three hand-like feet strongly aligned in front of him.

A gust of wind rattled through the leaves on the tree.

Mirg cleared his throat. The babbling, bagpipe sounds from the haggises gradually lowered to a murmur, before falling to a whisper and then silence as all ginger-red, fur-clad faces turned towards Mirg in anticipation. Their large, round eyes fixed on Mirg's eyes: their mouths tightly closed and their small pointed ears angled forward, ready to listen.

'Have I missed anything?'

All heads turned sharply towards Angus as he catapulted himself from the McMail burrow and tumbled into the crowd, knocking some of the other haggises over.

Jock sighed impatiently but Mirg spoke encouragingly before Jock could hurl insults at poor, hapless Angus.

'If you're quite ready, Angus - we'll begin the meeting.' Mirg remained his usual calm and placid self and smiled towards the back of the crowd.

Angus picked himself up off the ground and a number of grunts followed as he apologised to those around him. Dishevelled and feeling slightly embarrassed, he turned and faced Mirg. At least he hadn't missed anything.

CHAPTER THREE

The Bothy

Brodie tripled up the peaty burrow towards The Bothy muttering in discontent. He hated it in there. The sounds of innocent haggisen laughter grew louder as he made his way to the large, underground cavern where the air was slightly stale. Tree roots, entwined around one another, lined the cavern like a large network of blood vessels and a couple of fat roots that were growing straight down into the middle of the cavern were being used for a swing. A few of the mothers were watching over the young haggisen who were blissfully unaware of what was happening outside as they skipped and jumped around The Bothy with their friends. The older ones were either huddled together in little groups gossiping about their peers or joining in with the fun. Brodie stood for a few, pensive moments and watched his mother nurture some of the haggisen before tripling over to her.

'How long are we here for Mum?' he asked, already beginning to feel bored.

'As long as it takes. Now go and supervise some of the younger ones and play leap-haggis or hopscotch with them. Occupy yourself and you'll feel less bored.'

Brodie sighed restlessly and rolled his eyes. He looked at the groups of gossiping haggisen and decided that it wasn't for him. They were probably gossiping about him anyway.

'Holly McHaggis? Ah - there you are! You're needed over here - I think we've got another injury. A clash of heads during a game of Haggis Bulldogs,' said Grear McBrewster hurriedly as she concentrated on nursing a tearful young haggis in the sick bay.

'Oh dear,' said Holly and nudged Brodie towards the centre of The Bothy. 'On you go Brodie. Play games with the little ones and make sure that they don't hurt themselves. Jings Mc-Crackerty, we've enough injuries already for one day,' she said looking towards the sick bay where more tearful haggisen were joining the queue. Holly had a special gift of being able to nurse injuries and replace the tears with smiles. She was admired for her ability to turn what seemed a tragedy into something less painful and more positive. There was always enough of her warm heart to go around.

Brodie's top lip curled as he moved towards the young haggisen. Anything but this, he thought. Then he heard quarrelling voices. His ear twitched like a radar and turned 130 degrees to the left as he listened in.

'Did too!'

'Did not!'

'Too!!'

'Not, not, not!'

'Did too, you disgusting, stinking haggis!' screamed Kyla McHarris. Saunders McRancid laughed at her menacingly as she tucked her nose into her armpit. 'You're not supposed to do that in here you disgusting, smelly …'

Brodie read the signs and immediately dived between Saunders and Kyla to avert a snarling, fur-flying haggis fight. They could get pretty nasty.

THWACK!

Brodie saw a flash of light. Then everything went black as he fell to the ground. His head felt as though it had been split in two.

'S-s-sorry Brodie. I didn't see you - that head butt was meant for that filthy haggis there,' Kyla whined, screwing her face up tightly like she'd just sucked on a lemon.

Feeling dazed, Brodie groaned and rubbed his head. 'Ok … ok, enough!' he said, staggering back to his feet and shaking his head to get rid of the twittering birds that seemed to be flying around inside it. He squinted his eyes at Kyla and wondered how something so delicate looking could pack such a punch. Then he looked at the evil glint in Saunders' eyes.

'Saunders - you know you shouldn't do that to your friends, especially inside! You know it's only meant to ward off midges …' Brodie coughed hard. His nostrils were immediately overpowered with the strong, acrid smell; his eyes crossed and the fur on his face formed tight curls as he coughed again.

Saunders stared challengingly at Brodie and his mouth formed a crooked smile.

Brodie glared back at him through glassy eyes. If his head didn't hurt so much, he'd have head-butted Saunders himself.

Saunders burst into uncontrollable laughter as he watched Brodie recover.

'Something wrong?'

The grin on his face disappeared like a burst balloon when he heard the gruff voice of Bruce McSpruce. Saunders turned slowly towards him and felt himself sink into the peaty ground at the sight of Bruce towering above him on three long and very powerful looking legs.

Bruce liked to help out in The Bothy and disruptive haggisen knew to behave when he was about. Who wouldn't? He flashed a deathly grin before shovelling Saunders up in one arm and marching him down a darker burrow to The Delinquent's Corner where he would have to listen to a long lecture on how to behave. 'Next time, make sure you leave that smell for midges … if it happens again, why I'll knock you into the next universe, but I don't think there'll be a next time - will there Saunders?'

Saunders merely whimpered.

Kyla and Brodie giggled as they heard his whimpers trailing off down the burrow.

'You ok?' Brodie asked, turning to face Kyla.

Kyla flashed her sun-golden eyes at Brodie and smiled gratefully, coughing once or twice to clear her lungs. 'Thanks Brodie.' Her mouth formed a delicate heart shape as she smiled back at him.

Brodie felt a pleasant sensation form in his stomach.

'Come on Kyla, I thought you were supposed to be helping me with leap-haggis,' shouted Vanora McTavish as she marched towards them, 'not slacking off!'

The pleasant feeling in Brodie's stomach suddenly turned to dread.

Kyla stiffened at the piercing voice and looked under her eyes as Vanora's determined frame came into view. The ground quivered under each purposeful stomp. Kyla knew it was useless trying to explain what had happened. Vanora never listened - just strutted about the place and ordered everyone around. And her penetrating eyes could scare the spikes off a hedgehog so nobody really challenged her.

'Sorry Brodie - must go,' Kyla said apologetically and scuttled timidly after Vanora.

Brodie sighed as he watched them disappear into the mass of rowdy haggisen who remained ignorant to the rising tensions outside. His thoughts returned to the meeting and his growing anxiety ate away at him as he wondered why the meeting was so important.

Brodie scanned his eyes around The Bothy before taking a few steps back into the shadows. After about five minutes, when nobody had noticed him missing, he took a few more steps back and turned into the darkness of the burrow. The pinhole of light grew steadily larger as he sped through the burrow until daylight splashed into his face. Brodie crept just feet from the burrow's entrance and cocked his ear to listen to Mirg McVey's strained voice above the continuing panicked babble from the crowd.

CHAPTER FOUR

The Rowan Tree

'Look, it's not the first time this sort of thing has happened. One of our haggisen disappears for a few hours and we immediately think it's the evil forces,' said Mirg with slight unease. 'But, if you all care to remember, they always return - just strayed a bit too far and forgotten the time. Let's not be too hasty at this stage. If he isn't back by sunset, then we need to question what has happened to him. If he has strayed into the evil forces,' Mirg's misty-grey eyes grew dark and his voice took on a serious tone, 'then we'll have to think about what to do and how to protect ourselves. Until then, I'm remaining positive. I'm sure he'll be close by. And ... well ... we all know that Iron McGillis likes to play pranks, ' he said coughing a laugh.

A stocky haggis stepped forward from the crowd. 'Explain yourself! What do you mean he likes to play pranks?' There was fierce anger in Uisdean McGillis's voice as he shouted above the increasingly annoying babble. 'Will you lot just shut up so that I can hear myself think!' he demanded with his usual bluntness as he glared around at the crowd.

A gasp filtered from the crowd at such rudeness but was quickly followed by silence. Without even a word of thanks, Uisdean turned back to Mirg and continued to rant.

'My son is ...'

'Your son is nothing but a nuisance,' said Hamish McTosh, a very old and retired member of the Haggis Community Council. He was standing in the centre of the crowd and was wearing a casual, no nonsense expression on his face. His voice was cool and raspy. 'If it was anyone else, then I'd have to say that they *were* in trouble. But your son is a well-known prankster!' Hamish smiled soberly around the hushed crowd.

Uisdean McGillis's fur bristled, his thick, curly eyebrows knitted together in a frown and his ears swept back in anger as he turned to face Hamish. 'What would an old codger like you know about haggisen anyway - you've never had any!'

The crowd gasped against the silence. Uisdean continued to glare at Hamish. A glare that would seriously challenge Vanora McTavish's.

Hamish rolled his eyes and sighed contentedly as he shook his head dismissively. He was too old to be bothered with arguments and petty squabbles and as his eyesight was fading fast, a glare was wasted on him. 'Well, Uisdean. It's about time you realised that Iron is just an attention seeker. I bet my bare hide that he'll come waltzing in over the horizon shortly to see us all gathered here and worrying about him.' Hamish smiled gallantly and moved his eyes towards Jock and Mirg who were standing, open-mouthed.

The community nodded in agreement, although remained cautious of Uisdean.

A deep, clicking sound came from Uisdean's mouth as he began to grind his teeth. Steam began to rise from his flared nostrils. 'HOW. DARE. YOU!'

Everyone's ears swept back as though a gale force wind had blown against their faces.

'I say that the evil forces have got him! How do we know that the Silent Protector really works. Huh?' Uisdean looked to the crowd for support.

Their ears relaxed forward. Some haggises nodded in agreement, some shook their heads and others just stood blinking silently, unsure of whether to agree or disagree.

'None of us really knows what evil forces these trees are protecting us from,' said Mirg intelligently as he patted the trunk of the rowan tree next to him, 'but history tells us that we must have faith in them. Nothing evil has ever happened to us - right?'

The haggises nodded and shuffled, muttering their approval.

'Our burrows all exit near rowan trees and there are plenty of them scattered over the landscape. We never stray beyond a few metres of one, never go near the forests or swim in the loch,' he said scanning his eyes across the cluster of haggis heads.

'What about the witch?' snarled Uisdean, spit angrily foaming around the corners of his tightened mouth. A bitter smile twisted across his face as he noticed panic filling the crowd once again. Uisdean enjoyed nothing more than frightening others.

Jock stepped forward and raised a hand in the air. 'As long as we stay within the bounds of the Silent Protector, we will be safe. We may never have seen evil, and we don't really want to - do we?'

A strong murmur rattled around the crowd like a ball in a pinball machine and heads nodded and shook as thoughts were plainly divided.

'If Iron has wandered too far,' he said pausing momentarily, 'then we can only hope that no harm comes to him. We cannot put other lives at risk at this stage. If he hasn't returned soon, then we shall go out in groups to look for him - but not beyond our safety zone. Until then, I wish to remain positive.'

'Murderer!'

A deathly silence hung over Drumdrui. Every pair of startled haggis eyes turned and rested on Uisdean as he stood squarely in front of Mirg, his shoulders broad and his chest puffed out.

Brodie could hear a midge in the ensuing silence hiccupping contentedly after a hefty meal of rabbit blood. He knew that Uisdean's accusation was something he shouldn't have been listening to. The blood rushed to his face as his heart pounded against his chest, guilty of listening in, fearful of being discovered.

The hiccupping midge hovered around him, salivating at the

smell of the rushing blood. Brodie froze and held his breath as it continued to hover in front of his nose. His blood continued to storm through his body. The midge buzzed around his face for a few seconds, but simply let out a satisfying burp and flew on by. He'd been witness to hundreds of his friends being killed by the haggises' powerful odour. There was no way *he* was going to sink his vampire teeth into this haggis. Brodie was grateful. He would have been discovered for sure.

Mirg's eyes narrowed and he cleared his throat. 'Enough, enough! I just won't have you, Uisdean McGillis, disrupting the community in this way. I order you to silence during the remainder of this meeting and if you can't - you will be asked to leave.' This time, there was a definite tone to his voice that dared any haggis to defy.

Uisdean was about to ignore him and parted his lips to hotly protest but was interrupted by Rowena McBruan as she elbowed her way towards the front where Mirg was standing.

'Evil forces thistle-puffs! I found this tyke hiding behind the boulder up on the north face of the hill.' Her blubbery skin rippled under her ginger-red fur like a flowing river as she dragged Iron McGillis along with her.

'He was sniggering and rolling around in the heather laughing at every one of you,' she said, looking around the flabbergasted faces. Her large face jiggled like blancmange as she wheezed through her words. Iron kicked and spat at her, but his efforts were wasted. Rowena had him well and truly pegged in her blubbery hand.

'Delinquent.'

'Thoughtless.'

'Shame on him.'

The hisses and taunts continued as the crowd parted to let Rowena through. Iron flapped about as Rowena hauled him up by the scruff of the neck and launched him onto the stone at Mirg's eight-toed feet.

Brodie moved further up the burrow and hid in the shadows.

'Thank you, Rowena,' said Mirg in an air of calm and relief as he stared into Iron's, now frightened, eyes. He raised a hand into the air. 'And enough of the name calling. I won't tolerate that sort of behaviour from anyone.'

'How are you going to punish him?' a voice snarled from the depths of the crowd.

Silence fell around Drumdrui once again as every haggis stared at Mirg, waiting for an answer. He nodded to Jock.

Jock jumped down onto the ground, flipped a small stone over and grabbed a large, brown centipede between two of his talons before it could scuttle away.

The crowd groaned in horror.

Brodie's stomach lurched and he concealed a retch.

The centipede dangled helplessly from Jock's talons, all one hundred of its legs scrambling in mid air as Jock leapt back onto the stone and waved it in front of Iron's pale eyes.

Iron wailed, and buried his face in his shoulder. 'Dad, he can't! I fell asleep in the heather. Honest, Dad. I fell asleep in the heather. I was just coming back home when you called the meeting.'

Uisdean rushed forward. 'You heard him - he fell asleep. He can't be punished for falling asleep, he's no prankster!'

A muffle filtered around the crowd in disagreement with Uisdean.

'Would you like to take the punishment for your son then?' asked Mirg as he winked at Uisdean and smiled wryly.

Uisdean looked at his bawling son and looked back to Mirg.

Mirg looked at Uisdean and nodded towards Iron. The crowd tried to understand the sign language that the two haggises exchanged over the next few moments, but they were as perplexed as Jock McHaggis was.

Uisdean finally spoke to his son. 'Iron - you have had us all worried by your disappearance and all for what? A prank. You cannot cry wolf - the next time we won't really believe you're missing.' He paused briefly and fired a glare at Mirg. 'You know the rules of the land.'

Brodie shuddered and coughed as he cleared his throat of the imaginary centipede that was wriggling its way out of it. Iron wasn't one of his favourite haggises, but he somehow felt sorry for the bubbling heap that lay in front of him.

'Dad - really, I fell asleep. I promise I won't do it agaaaaaaaaaain,' he wailed as he squeezed his eyes shut, but the image of the centipede was still there, wriggling its legs in front of him.

Brodie surveyed the taut faces of the stunned crowed as they gulped slowly and tried to clear their throats. Haggises were strict vegetarians.

Iron pivoted his head back towards the crowd and apologised through a forced, almost angelic smile, revealing a row of crooked, yellow haggis teeth.

Feeling satisfied that Iron had learned his lesson, Mirg nodded to Uisdean and Jock. Jock quietly released the centipede from his grips and it scuttled down the side of the rock towards a clump of white heather. A large, black bird swooped down from the tree and snaffled the centipede before it could take cover.

'Well, young Iron. Let that be a lesson to you. Next time - it'll be three centipedes you'll be eating,' said Mirg feeling content that he could see some sort of remorse behind Iron's young eyes.

Iron stopped whining and pivoted his body to line up with his head before jumping down from the rock. Brodie crept further up the burrow and watched secretively as Iron scooted past him towards the McGillis burrow. He heard him continue to mutter his innocence about falling asleep in the heather.

A mixture of laughter and relief filtered through the crowd as each haggis went back to doing what they were before they were called together that afternoon. Witches and evil forces were words that were not repeated again. Even though Iron McGillis continued to protest his innocence for that day, he seemed to change from being a scallywag and a bully, well almost. He was found once or twice chasing the female haggisen through the heather and around rowan trees for a haggis snog as they fled in tears - but boys will be boys. Between Iron creating mayhem once in a while and Saunders McRancid leaving foul smells where he shouldn't - life became almost normal once again in Drumdrui.

*

On a morning towards the end of the summer, Brodie emerged from the McHaggis burrow before anybody else had risen, his mind full of unanswered questions. He sat and watched the beginning of one of the last days of summer. As the sun rose slowly from the horizon, everything around him, even the sky, turned a warm shade of red. The birds began chirping in the trees, rabbit tails bobbed about the hillside, and plants tilted their heads to kiss the morning sunshine.

Brodie tripled to the centre of Drumdrui and looked around at all the other burrows buried in the heather and the rowan trees that stood beside them. He'd never thought of it before the day Iron McGillis went missing, before all the panic about the Silent Protector. His eyes scanned the hillside and the rowan trees dotted across it and his face twisted into a frown as he pondered over the Silent Protector.

'Best time of the day, son, eh?'

Brodie's heart skipped a beat and he swung his head around on his body. 'You frightened me there, Dad.'

'Sorry Brodie, didn't mean to. You're up early.' Then his eyes narrowed suspiciously. 'What do you need to be frightened of anyway?'

Brodie's stomach lurched and he stepped his body around to face his father. 'Ach ... it was just so quiet and peaceful. I was admiring the trees ... that's all. Your voice was unexpected,' he said sheepishly. He had been more jumpy and more cautious of what was around him since that meeting in Drumdrui. He must never let his father find out that he had listened that day.

'Trees? Hmmm .... yes, beautiful, aren't they? The red berries make them look very heavy at this time of year. But you know they're poisonous, don't you?' said Jock in his normal, lecturing way.

Brodie yawned and scratched at his nose. 'Yes Dad, how could I not know,' he said trying to sound interested, remembering the countless times he'd been warned about them. He paused hesitantly before asking his father the question that had been burning inside him for the last ten weeks.

'How do we know that the rowan trees protect us? I mean, why do we think they do? In fact - what are they really protecting us from?'

Jock stiffened at Brodie's question. 'Son, all I know is that we've never been harmed by anything. Let's just get on with life as it is and don't interfere with what we don't know. Why the question?' he asked, sounding mystified.

Brodie's eyes lit up like light bulbs and took the question as an invitation to bombard his father with more questions. 'So what's beyond the Silent Protector?' The words were out before he thought about what he'd asked.

Jock's face turned thunderous and his eyes narrowed almost

to slits. 'Don't let me hear you say that again! Don't mess with the evil forces Brodie - understand? I don't know who's been filling your head with nonsense - but let it end, right here right now!' The conversation finished abruptly and Jock nudged Brodie in the shoulder as he made his way back to the McHaggis burrow.

The last ray of sun rose from the horizon and the landscape took on its rightful colour. Brodie nodded silently and followed his father back to the burrow. But his intrigue had no means of stopping and anticipation rose high in his chest as he munched on a breakfast of nettles and wild berries. He began to formulate a plan on how to find the answers he was looking for. But he had to be careful not to get caught.

CHAPTER FIVE

Mystery in the Loch

Summer gave way to autumn with gusting winds stealing leaves off trees and littering them around the countryside. The hills took on a purple tinge as the autumn heather bloomed. Brodie and Macca McRoberts ran hard along the peaty path for about a mile, then left it and twisted their way through the heather, not stopping until they reached the brow of Darmaeddie hill. A welcoming, cool breeze wafted over Brodie's sweat-drenched fur and he smiled widely at the loch unfolding southwards towards the horizon. To him, it looked different each day with a new story to tell.

'You're not serious about going in there for a swim?' said Macca seeing the urge swell in Brodie's blue eyes. 'Don't you know that a kelpie lives in that loch? No hoggin has ever swum in there.'

'How do you know there's a kelpie in there?'

'Because ... well ... because ...'

'Because our folks claim that there's a kelpie hiding in there, that's why. Nobody's seen one, so how do we even know that it exists, never mind what it looks like?' Brodie moved down the hillside towards the rippling water. Macca galloped after him.

'It's big. Ugly. Mean. It'll eat you. And there are no trees out there - look,' he said urging Brodie back to his senses as he pointed across the glistening water. 'If you swim out there, there are no trees close to you. Don't be so stupid.'

Brodie didn't look. He blew the puffball off an innocent thistle and watched the feathery pieces flutter delicately to the ground before wrapping his jaws around the thistle head and biting it off its stem. After crunching his way through the juicy snack, he smiled a toothy grin and pushed a leg under Macca's fluted nose, balancing evenly on the other two.

'I've thought of that,' he said proudly displaying a plait of very fine rowan wood fastened tightly around his ankle. 'I've been working at it for weeks now, stripping thin rowan branches with my teeth and plaiting the strips, but these made it tricky. Kept getting tied in knots,' he said staring stupidly at his, slightly webbed toe-like fingers.

'I'm now ready to stray further than any other haggis has done. I need to prove a point - either there is something out there or there isn't. Won't know until I've tried it.'

Macca looked on horrified. 'What if it doesn't work - I mean, what if it's more than just the rowan wood - what if you need the whole tree? What if it doesn't work in water? What if you get caught by your Dad? He'll make you eat insects!' he said, screwing his face up tightly. 'You could ... you could ... get killed! YOU'RE CRAZY!'

'Don't be so stupid,' said Brodie. 'Somebody needs to find out some truths and the only way is for me to swim out there.' He pointed towards the horizon where the folds of mountains paled into the distance beyond the loch.

The colour drained from Macca's crystal-blue eyes and his pupils formed horizontal slits as his numb gaze traced the line of Brodie's talon. His voice croaked through a dry throat. 'There could be anything out there ... y-y-you can't really be serious?'

A cool defiance glinted in Brodie's eyes and the corners of his leathery, brown mouth curled into a crooked smile. 'Deathly serious. But you're to tell no one - understand? No one.' Brodie's cold tones were carried away in the breeze.

'But ...'

'But nothing - you have to give me your word. I've told you in confidence.'

Macca nodded reluctantly. 'But, you can't. You'll get

killed!'

'Nonsense!' said Brodie sharply, but the knot in his stomach tightened. He knew that Macca could be right.

*

Two very long weeks passed before Brodie finally managed to escape on his own for a full day. Brodie never wished illness on anyone, but he heaved a sigh of relief when he heard that Macca had been confined to barracks because of a bad haggis cold, which could last anything from a week to a few months. Ever since he had confided in Macca about his plan to swim out into the loch, Macca had followed him around like his shadow. Only, Macca didn't disappear when the sun was blotted out by clouds or when night fell. He lingered more than a bad smell; more like a biting midge on his skin that he just couldn't shake off - until today.

The sky was almost an endless blue, with a few faint wisps of autumn cloud. Small, circular ripples formed on the glittering surface of the water as silvery fish leapt high into the air and sucked up their prey of unwitting flies before diving effortlessly back into the water.

Brodie checked that the rowan-wood plait was secured tightly around his ankle. He raised his head towards the sky, smiled widely, and paused briefly before splashing clumsily into the water. An image of Macca's concerned eyes when Brodie had told him about his plan flashed before him. The sudden shock of the icy-coldness against his skin sent stabbing pains throughout his small body and he wondered then if he was doing the right thing. But as his fur captured a layer of water against his skin, it warmed to his body and he soon forgot about how cold he initially felt and how worried Macca's eyes had looked.

His odd-shaped body looked clumsy, but Brodie swam with

the grace of an otter, occasionally popping up to the surface for some air. It was a while before he looked back to see how far he had swum. The end of the loch where he had set out from was now barely visible. A large grin divided his ginger-red face and with excitement rushing through his veins, Brodie swam on. He dived below the surface and skimmed through the water with no fear of what might lie ahead of him. Beginning to feel a bit tired, he turned westwards and headed towards the shore for a rest.

'Whoa … whooooaaaaa … whooaaaaaaaaggh …' Brodie screamed as he was suddenly twisted around and around in a strong whirlpool, sucking him downwards into the loch. Water gushed up his four nostrils and into his nose, flooding his mouth and throat as he was tossed around like a leaf in a hurricane. His lungs began to fill up with water. They felt like exploding. He choked and spluttered as the force of the water kept sucking him downwards. He needed air and quick!

Brodie fought against the pressure of the whirlpool with everything that he had, but it was no use. He continued to be sucked deeper and deeper into the loch. His lungs were being crushed and all the time he wanted to breathe. His heart slowed down, begging for air to be pumped into his blood. And then, it all simply stopped. The pressure released and the water became calm once again.

Brodie crashed through the surface of the water and the cool fresh air preciously flooded his tired lungs. He violently coughed up water through desperate gasps of air. His breathing was quick and shallow. With only the strength of a baby left, he paddled to the shore where he lay and rested for a while.

'What was that?' he said in a strangled voice, clawing at his chest and throat as he continued to cough water from his lungs.

'Where … how …?' He sat up and stared determinedly across the gleaming water, trying to make sense of what had just happened. But apart from a small ripple from the breeze, there was nothing out of the ordinary to be seen. His eyes squinted northwards as he tried to focus on home. It was too far away. He was too weak to swim home. And too scared.

A sudden flash of rainbow-coloured light in the water jolted his concentration and another whirlpool whipped up the loch. Brodie's heart pounded hard against his chest. He looked on in horror at the water twisting around and around, like it was draining down a plughole. Then it stopped, leaving the loch calm and almost untouched.

'What on earth ...?' Brodie edged closer to the water and waited, the blood pumping fast around his body. He sat like a statue, watching, waiting. In fear of something coming out of the water. But nothing happened for some time.

Then it was there again. The rainbow-coloured light flashed across the surface of the water, quickly followed by a whirlpool.

Brodie shuddered and darted back up the shore, launching himself behind a boulder like a snake was biting at his heels. Should he go back for a closer look or just swim for home? New energy flowed through his veins as he lay in wait.

But his curiosity was too much. After a few more quiet moments, Brodie edged back to the loch. Cautiously, like a crocodile stalking his prey, he slipped into the water. The shore dipped away sharply and the loch became dark and bottomless. He breathed in deeply, filling his small lungs with fresh, autumn air, and dived down, down, down against the jagged rock face until it became too dark to see anything. He waited for a few moments. Everything was murky.

FLASH!

The rainbow colours lit up the loch.

The colourful rays danced in the water and immediately captivated Brodie's eyes.

Something moved. Something very large.

Brodie's heart banged hard against his chest and a cold terror washed through him. His lungs were desperate for air but he couldn't move up or down. He was frozen with fear.

The rock face changed shape and began moving towards him. Closer and closer.

Something else moved. It looked green under the dancing kaleidoscope of colours as it gradually emerged from the rock. A nose, then an eye the size of a football. It was like nothing he'd ever imagined. The pounding of blood as it rushed around his head was all that he could hear.

A whirlpool formed just metres from him as the large, green form just kept spewing out of the rock face. Each of its scaly webbed feet dwarfed him, and its tail went on forever. Brodie pressed himself against the rock face and watched every lasting piece of the green form flow into the loch. When the tip of its tail emerged from the rock, the rainbow colour vanished leaving the water its usual dark and peaty brown colour. The whirlpool stopped.

Brodie paced the small, pebbly shore as he regained his breath after his rapid retreat from the water.

'I don't believe what I've just seen. Is that a kelpie? What else could it be?' A cool wind blew across his saturated haggis fur. He shivered and looked out across the loch as he continued to debate with himself.

'Why hasn't anyone else seen it?'

'What do I do next?'

'Get the others?'

'No, no, no, they'll never believe me.' He paced up and down the pebbly shore, bursting with anxiety.

'Oh, what to do? I could swim home now and come back tomorrow. But what for? Why not now?' he said nodding his furry head. His ears twitched in excited panic and all twenty-four toe-like fingers drummed against the ground as he pondered over what to do.

The wind blew across his face. It had turned sharp. The sun began to lower in the west and the clouds took on a darkened tinge. It was getting late. The few remaining leaves blowing on the rowan trees seemed to be whispering a message of warning to him. There seemed to be more rustling noise from the leaves than there were leaves.

Brodie felt his chest tighten as the seeds of a plan began to take root. He looked about him and noted the way everything was. After he was certain that he would find the place again tomorrow, he plunged into the water and swam for home. He was scared, but strangely satisfied. He fumbled at his ankle. The rowan plait was still in tact.

It took him much longer to swim back to Darmaeddie than he thought it would. The last sliver of light across the horizon was being pushed out by the evening sky. He was late. Very, very late.

CHAPTER SIX

The Kelpie

'You lost something? You've been in and out of that burrow at least four times in the last wee while.'

Jock spun round nervously as Hamish McTosh's voice jumped out of the darkness at him. He hadn't noticed the old haggis sitting under the now almost leafless rowan tree that stood in the centre of Drumdrui.

Hamish nodded towards the last splinter of light in the sky as it was enveloped by the darkness. 'Aye, the nights are fair drawing in. Soon be winter.' He stood up and balanced on two of his wobbling legs while he stretched the third one up into the air, then he did the same with the other two and let out a large sigh.

'I hate these long, dark winters. They do nothing for my creaking old bones. We need to do something in the winters instead of sleeping as soon as the darkness comes in. What do you reckon Jock?'

'Yes, you're right there Hamish. Maybe we can talk about it tomorrow. Good night,' Jock said abruptly and tripled back into the burrow in the hope that Hamish would go home. No sooner was he inside when he heard a thud followed by a muffled howl.

'It's Brodie,' said Holly as she pushed past Jock with eyes as wide as saucers.

'Jock? Are you still therrrre?'

Both Jock and Holly exchanged uneasy glances and rushed outside. They stared down at Hamish's mangled body. He'd taken a tumble and had landed with his legs wrapped around his body. Holly moved around the tangled mess to find Hamish's face. He was grinning childishly and his eyes glistened dazedly.

'Why Hamish McTosh. You've been eating those

dandelions again, haven't you?'

Hamish's stupid grin grew wider.

'Holly, keep your voice down - we don't want the others knowing. We need to get him back to his burrow now.'

'How do you propose we do that? Normally we'd leave him where he fell over to sleep it off.'

'But we can't - not tonight. Brodie's missing.'

Hamish's bagpipe-like laughs filtered into the still, night air.

'Hamish - will you be quiet,' said Jock in a strained whisper.

'Brodie - missing? Not another Iron McGillis, ha, ha, ha. And this time YOUR son, ha, ha, ha. Better not let Uisdean find out, hee, hee, ha, ha.'

'Those dandelions make haggises laugh at the strangest of things,' said Holly as she clasped her hand around one of his ankles. Jock stuffed a fistful of grass into Hamish's mouth to shut him up and grabbed another ankle, and between them, they eventually managed to drag him back to his burrow where they left him snoring contentedly.

'His drunken stupor would suggest that he's eaten a fair quantity of dandelions. At least he won't remember Brodie missing in the morning. I hope none of us do,' said Holly in a worried whisper which penetrated Jock like an arrow through his chest. 'He's long overdue. What could've happened to him?'

'I don't know, but I've got to go out and find him. I'll try the loch first.'

'Be careful Jock. It's so dark,' said Holly dropping her voice even lower. But he had already gone. He sped down the burrow, through the centre of Drumdrui and up the hillside towards the loch.

Wheezing and puffing breathlessly, Brodie crawled from the loch and flopped himself down on the grass, exhausted after the hard swim back. His mind flashed back to the massive green thing he'd seen emerging from the rock. Then his thoughts returned to how late he was and how the entire community would be gathered to discuss his disappearance. How was he going to explain it? But he was so consumed with curiosity and mounting excitement that no amount of punishment or eating of insects could stop him from going back to find out more.

Something stirred in the dark loch. Brodie gasped and stared at the water, fear running through his eyes as he cocked his head to listen. Everything went quiet. With his eyes still fixed on the water, he reached down to his ankle, untied the rowan tree plait and hid it under the heather beside a large, lichen-covered stone.

He stood for a few silent moments, listening, watching as he picked at the white lichen on the stone. There it was again. Something stirred in the water. Every piece of fur on his body stood on end and a cold shiver ran through him. He leapt over the stone and fled up the hillside towards home, never daring to look back. But it was dark. He couldn't see well through the heather. Whatever he hit was solid and badly winded him. The ground jumped up to meet his face as he tumbled into the darkness, heather poking at his eyes and thistles stabbing at his skin before he splashed into the burn.

'Brodie?'

'Dad?'

'Thank goodness you're safe.'

'Thank goodness it's you, Dad. I've been …' said Brodie as he began stammering his way through an excuse. He stumbled through the water as it flowed past him on its way down the hillside towards the loch and suddenly realised that falling into the burn had turned out to be a fortunate excuse for why he was so wet.

'Hold your tongue until we get home, laddie. We mustn't let anyone see us arriving back at Drumdrui. We'll sneak in over the top and down the east side.'

Brodie was confused at his father's stealthy behaviour, but did as he was instructed. When they arrived back at Drumdrui, they were met with the steady snore from sleeping haggises. Which is why no birds nested in the trees for miles around - they found it impossible to sleep with that racket going on. Brodie snuck into the McHaggis burrow, pleased to be back home. Jock glanced around secretively before following Brodie. For a split second, he thought he saw a shadow move over at the McGillis burrow.

*

Winter had taken firm root and the icy, north winds raged around Drumdrui as all haggises curled up and semi-hibernated to avoid the squally, wintry showers. Brodie had been like a prisoner, not being allowed out of his father's sight since the night he returned home late. He couldn't so much as breathe the wrong way and he was questioned. Nobody had suspected that Brodie had disappeared. He had told his father that he had simply fallen asleep in the heather. Jock had accepted the excuse, but had sworn Brodie to secrecy in fear of being thrown off the Council for not having control of his son. Hamish McTosh hadn't remembered a thing after his night on the dandelions, which was of great relief to Jock and Holly.

It wasn't unusual for everyone to feel uneasy in the company of Uisdean McGillis - but Brodie had felt particularly uneasy of late, often catching Uisdean surveying him with great interest out of his sly, untrusting eyes. Uisdean would simply return a slow, twisted smile to Brodie and make a deep, chuckling sound in his throat forcing Brodie to shudder and look away quickly.

'There's a storm brewing,' said Jock lifting his head as he munched on some of the dead bracken. Its burnt-orange colour camouflaged them well against the hillside.

The others lifted their oval heads from the bracken and followed Jock's gaze to the Monarch of the Glen, standing strong and powerful at the top of the hill, his head tilted as he breathed in the wind. The cold air formed strong rings of moisture as it bellowed from the stag's large nostrils. He looked down the hillside and eyed the haggises sternly, then raised his head and breathed in the air again. His antlers looked heavy and cumbersome, like two leafless trees on his head.

'Aye - he's sniffing the air. Sure to be a storm on its way. We should get back,' said Athol McDermitt, mumbling around a mouthful of tasty bracken.

Every haggis nodded in agreement and began herding their way down the hillside to safety, munching on the last of their lunchtime snack as they went. Brodie paused and looked back to the Monarch of the Glen. About a hundred or so deer and stags now surrounded him as they watched the haggises with their stern, dark eyes. There was an aura of power about the large stag that Brodie admired. Then, in an instant, the animals turned quickly and leapt their way through the bracken until they had disappeared over the top of the hill.

A clap of thunder followed and a sudden strong gust of wind knocked Vanora McTavish backwards off her feet and she landed heavily on wee Kyla McHarris. Others rallied around and pushed the large haggis back to her feet. Leaning heavily into the wind, the haggises continued their way down the hillside, Kyla feeling a bit flatter than she had a few moments ago.

Large, wintry clouds whipped across the frozen sky. The wind strengthened to gale force and tried beating the haggises back up the hillside. The sky lit up with a flash of lightening and was quickly followed by a deafening roll of thunder and a sudden lashing of horizontal hailstones.

'Quick - get in the McMail burrow. Hurry!' Mirg's voice

was whipped away by the violent wind as the hail beat hard against his face. 'Who knows which way to go when we're in there?'

'I do,' said Jock hurriedly. 'I spent last summer in them with Angus.'

'You did?' Mirg sounded surprised.

'Yes - and it's going to help us now. So quick you lot. Keep close.' Jock nipped into the burrow and was followed by a chain of haggises, all babbling at their excitement of being allowed in the McMail burrow and getting out of the storm. After Mirg had herded half of the group into the burrow, he joined the middle of the chain to keep it moving and instructed Brodie to take over and then follow on at the rear to make sure that nobody was left behind.

'And watch out for Angus McMail - he doesn't look where he's going and won't expect to find us in here.'

Brodie nodded as he took over from Mirg and ensured that everyone made it safely into the burrow. Saunders McRancid was the last haggis to enter the burrow. A malicious grin flitted across his face.

'Don't even think about it,' Brodie instructed as he did one final sweep of the hillside with his crystal-blue eyes. But Brodie could barely see beyond his nose through the blizzard. He was cold and soaked to the skin and welcomed the warmth of the burrow and the contented haggis babble that filtered down to him as he followed on at the rear.

The snow on Brodie's fur began to melt and it irritated him as it trickled down his head and into his eyes. After a few moments, he stopped to shake the snow from his head and clear his eyes. When he looked up, he saw Saunders' backside bobbing up and down just before it faded into the darkness. With a sudden feeling of loneliness, he sped through the burrow to catch up before he lost everyone.

THWACK!

Brodie was rammed into the side of the burrow at high speed.

*

Brodie didn't know how long he had lain unconscious for. Groaning through sleepiness and pain, he looked around himself. Angus McMail lay in a heap next to him.

'A-Angus? You alright Angus?'

There was no response.

Brodie rubbed his chest where Angus had hurtled into him. It was tender, but he managed to stagger to his feet as the feeling slowly flowed back into his limbs. He pushed Angus with his foot and shouted in his ear.

'ANGUS! ARE YOU OK?'

There was still no response. Angus lay very still, apart from the gentle rise and fall of his chest. He began to snore - contentedly. It could be hours before he regained consciousness. Brodie had to get some help. He walked slowly along the burrow until the pain in his body eased and allowed him to work up a bit of speed. But it was by no means fast. The burrow took a sharp left and then broke into a three-way junction.

'Which one? Which one do I take?' Brodie stared at the first burrow, then the middle one, then the third one. They all looked the same. He ran back to Angus - he was still snoring loudly. He ran back to the junction and looked from one burrow to the next then took a snap decision to go into the middle burrow.

'If it's the wrong one, then I'll come back and try another one,' he muttered beginning to feel slightly panicked. Would his father ever believe this excuse for being late?

The burrow came to another three-way junction. It was turning into a bigger maze than he'd thought and he imagined himself running around in there for days. Little wonder nobody was allowed in the McMail network - they could starve to death before they got out!

Brodie took the middle burrow again and ran as fast as his injuries would allow him to. A pinhole of light came into view. At least he was getting out - but he didn't know where.

The storm was still furiously whipping around the hillside, blasting snow and hail into every crevice it could find. A small pile of snow had partially formed over the entrance to the burrow. Brodie pushed some of the snow away and poked his head out into the storm. He was at Darmaeddie Loch. The water was dark and fierce-looking as the winds lashed it against the shore.

Something suddenly seized the fur on Brodie's shoulder hauling him out of the burrow and into the snow. As he rolled over, and over, and over again along the ground, the snow stuck to his fur and turned him into a ball of snow. He eventually crashed into the stone at the side of the loch and the snow broke up and fell away from his body. He remained lying on his back for a few moments and stared up at the snow whipping around the sky above him. Then he rolled onto his side and looked back towards the burrow to see what had attacked him. His mouth fell open in horror.

A hideous, crooked-looking figure was standing in front of the burrow, saliva dripping from its rotting teeth. Its black hair was in matted clumps all over its twisted body of rotting, black skin.

Brodie rubbed the snow from his eyes to make sure what he was seeing was real.

The black, coal-like eyes of the creature stared mercilessly back at Brodie as he lay in the snow, shivering, frightened and confused. It thrust out a knobbly, hairless fist and pointed a twisted, black nail at him as it spoke in a deep and gurgly voice.

'At last - I've managed to capture a haggissss.'

Even though the creature was sickeningly ugly, Brodie felt strangely compelled to stare at its twisted and repulsive form.

'What do you mean, and what ... who are you?' he asked in anguish.

The wind swirled the snow around them and drifted it into the burrow, almost blocking it up completely.

'The kelpie that your father has warned you about. You shouldn't have swum in the loch, Brodie McHaggissss. You shouldn't have.'

A jolt seemed to hit him in the back of the head and he hastened to respond to the kelpie. 'B-b-but … if you're the kelpie … what was that other thing I saw?'

'Who cares - you shouldn't have swum in MY loch.'

A wave of cold fear swept through Brodie's body.

Snow and hail blasted against the kelpie as he dragged his feet through the snow. If it was possible, he seemed to turn uglier the closer he got to Brodie.

Brodie felt a violent tug behind his navel.

'You're a fairly ugly beastie, I have to sssssay,' the kelpie hissed as the snow crunched under his bunion encrusted, mouldy feet. A crease formed between his bulbous, black eyes and mucus oozed from the twisted knot he had for a nose. His eyes were severely uneven and his mouth slanted in the opposite direction as though one side of his face had melted.

Something inside Brodie overpowered him. Standing up in his defence, he faced the kelpie squarely. 'You're calling ME ugly? Have you looked at yourself lately?'

The kelpie stiffened at Brodie's words and he remained motionless for a few seconds. His face twisted into more contortion. A blood-red ring formed around his eyes and he seemed to grow larger.

Brodie could hear the blood pumping in his ears as his heart beat faster than it ever had. He turned and dived into the heather where he'd left his plait of rowan wood and fumbled his toe-like fingers around the ground as he struggled to find it.

The kelpie's footsteps drew closer.

Brodie's fingers brushed across the plait. He grabbed it, but it was stuck. He tugged at it several times, but it wouldn't budge. Then he gave one hard jerk and the plait broke free sending Brodie tumbling on his back with his three feet protruding from the heather. Snapping his legs back in, he up-righted himself and hurriedly tied the plait around his ankle before leaping out of the heather.

A large, repulsive black horse stood facing Brodie with the same knot of a nose and blood-red eyes as the kelpie. Its skin looked to be rotting and its mane resembled seaweed.

Brodie stared in shock at the transformed kelpie as it snorted angrily at him and bared three rows of severely rotten teeth. He weighed up his odds of managing to get back to the burrow. They were slim. Very slim. His only other option was the loch. He turned and looked at the freezing cold water being whipped around in the storm. It was his only way out. He leapt from the shore, splashed into the water and swam as hard and as furious as he could, but the storm did its best to slow him down, sapping at his energy.

The kelpie dived into the water after him.

It was a race against time. Brodie didn't know where he was going, he just had to swim for his life. It was quicker than going over ground and it was taking the danger away from home. His limbs began to tire as he swam on and on through the storm. But the kelpie gained on his every stroke. His efforts were fruitless. He stiffened with fear when the kelpie seized his ankle and dragged him down, down, down into the cold depths of the loch.

The kelpie's grasp was too strong for him. He had no means of escape. The Silent Protector hadn't helped him. Macca was right - the kelpie would eat him, probably alive. His energy left him completely and he faded in and out of consciousness as the kelpie dragged him down.

CHAPTER SEVEN

The Secret of Loch Ness

The cold water began to swirl and spun Brodie and the kelpie around in circles, dragging them both further down into the loch.

The vortex! Brodie regained consciousness as he quickly realised where he was. There was little time left to escape. He kicked his foot hard against the kelpie's firm grip.

The vortex continued to twist them around and around.

Brodie kicked hard again. The kelpie's grip loosened and he kicked free. The water gushed up his nose and into his lungs. He felt he was drowning.

Then the swirling suddenly stopped - just as before - just as Brodie thought it would. He wasted no time in scrabbling to the surface. The wind and snow lashed against him as he gasped hungrily for air. He had to get to safety. An icy shudder ran through Brodie as he bobbed up and down in the water, his legs suddenly feeling vulnerable as they dangled in the depths of the loch like bait. After filling his lungs with the cold, wintry air, he dived back into the water. The kelpie was nowhere to be seen as he sped through the brown-tinged water towards the rock face.

FLASH!

The rainbow colours momentarily lit up the loch. Brodie peered through the peaty water as he looked for the large, green creature emerging from the rock, so it almost scared every strand of fur off his skin when the creature approached from behind him and this time went into the rock face. As soon as the tip of its long tail disappeared behind the rock, the rainbow light faded and the vortex came to an abrupt halt.

Brodie hurriedly swam after the creature and slammed into the rock. He was grateful that the water slowed things down as it softened the blow to his head. Slightly dazed, he tried again, but it was no use. There was no opening. It just didn't make sense. He swam to the surface and rushed more cold air into his lungs before descending the rock face again.

The loch lit up once again and two more of the huge, green forms glided effortlessly towards the rock face. A small opening appeared and seemed to adjust itself around the first creature, growing larger where it had to and almost closing off as soon as the tip of its tail entered the rock. The second one followed and the rock face opened up again. Brodie saw his opportunity and swam in beside the creature's large fin, careful not to get whacked by it as the creature gently glided through the water and through the rock.

He was in. A sudden wave of dread flushed through Brodie's veins as he saw the hole in the rock close behind him. Ok, so he'd shaken off the kelpie, but for all he knew worse could lie in front of him. He could be trapped forever. For the first time that he could remember, he wished he wasn't filled with so much curiosity and was more normal and accepted things as they were. He was just too inquisitive for his own good.

The rainbow light grew more intense as Brodie continued to swim along the tunnel with the huge creatures in their own hidden world. The tunnel eventually opened out into a massive expanse of water. Brodie drew up to the side and quietly broke the surface of the water. His mouth fell open and he lapsed into a giddy pleasure at the sight before him.

The brightly coloured rock that lined the large cavern twinkled high above his head. Rainbow striped stalactites of varying lengths hung stylishly from the roof and echoes rang around the cavern from the water that was purposefully dripping from each one onto the stalagmites below. It was a place of pure beauty and serenity. Brodie closed his mouth, scrambled from the water and shook himself like a dog would to get most of the water off his fur.

Transfixed and with his head angled upwards, he gasped at the hidden beauty as he splashed his way around the marbled floor of the cavern. A noise from the water stirred him out of his concentration.

'How did a wee critter like you get in here?'

Brodie swung his head around on his body and looked back to the water. 'Huh?'

'Yes, you there with the fur on - how did you get in here? This is private property!' Two familiar green eyes, the size of footballs, stared at Brodie from the water. 'Kelpie got your tongue?'

Brodie stepped around to face the stern eyes. 'I … I … was escaping from the kelpie,' he said nervously.

'You managed to escape? Aren't you the lucky one? I'm surprised he didn't drown you lot years ago. My great grandmother banished you to the other end of the loch because she couldn't put up with your intolerable snoring!'

Seal-like laughter filled the cavern as a number of other large, green heads rose from the rainbow-drenched water. Brodie blushed and edged back into the cavern, away from the creatures. He really wasn't so sure that he was out of danger yet.

A deeper, slightly clicking voice came from the water. 'Thought you were all told not to swim in the loch? What makes you so special? And answer the question - how'd you get in here?'

As Brodie stared at the large, green eyes, more and more pairs appeared above the water and blinked attentively at him. How was he going to escape? It was at that point he wondered if he would ever see the light of day again. He cleared his throat and surveyed the audience of football-sized eyes.

'I … I told you. I was escaping from the kelpie,' he said lowering his eyes to the marble floor to avoid the glares as he spoke through a pleading voice. 'Are you going to kill me?'

A low murmur filtered around the plesiosaurs as they moved

about in the water and discussed something that Brodie strained to hear. They returned their gaze to him.

'No, we won't, but we can hand you over to the kelpie who would do the honours! You shouldn't be here, young haggis.'

'Fairly ugly looking beastie too,' said one of the other plesiosaurs, snorting bubbles in the water. 'I'd heard they were, but seeing is believing. Yes sir-ee.'

In a matter of seconds, Brodie went from being scared to being totally confident as his short temper emerged again. He didn't take kindly to being called ugly. He knelt down to the water's edge and stared right into the eyes of the plesiosaur who had delivered the fatal words.

'Who are you calling ugly - looked at yourself lately?!' he screamed.

The dripping of water in the cavern was all that could be heard in the long silence that followed. Brodie's brow pushed back in fear as dozens of large, green eyes stared back at him. He gulped slowly.

Then an eruption of plesiosaur laughter echoed around the cavern.

'So small and yet so fearless. You've got to hand it to him. What's your name?'

Brodie looked cautiously around him before responding. 'Brodie. Brodie McHaggis,' he replied puffing out his chest as he straightened himself up on his three legs.

'Ah well, young Brodie. Your ancestors wanted to dismiss us as a myth. They wanted to frighten everybody from swimming in the loch so that nobody would find this place.' A female plesiosaur moved closer to Brodie and stretched her long, smooth neck above the water.

Brodie craned his neck upwards. Her skin was shiny and made up of zillions of small scales. 'Why? What is this place?' he asked cautiously.

'Our place. A place given to us by a mutual friend to escape danger … well, let's say that your ancestors were given this gift too and now you have it.'

A larger plesiosaur with dark green blemishes on his skin swam in beside her, butting her with his nose. 'Enough, Nessie. We shouldn't even be talking to him. He should be taken back to where he came from and told never to repeat a word of this.'

'Yeah, really? Like his ancestors were? Fat lot of good that did!'

'Well, in hundreds of years, only one little runt of a haggis has actually challenged the myths. Who's going to believe him anyway? They'll all think he's bonkers. He must go back now.'

Brodie parted his leathery lips and was about to protest when the cavern began to flicker a spangly green colour.

'Ooooh - the Northern Lights are out tonight - shall we go?' said Nessie smoothly, with an air of mischief in her voice as she turned her attention from Brodie.

'You know Nessie … we'll get caught one day - you know they've got this really fancy equipment that'll trap us,' said Ranald, a smaller plesiosaur.

'Not on a night like this - they'll never know.'

Brodie paced the marbled floor in confusion. 'Go where?'

The plesiosaurs had momentarily forgotten that he was even standing there and all swung around and fixed their gaze on him.

'Loch Ness of course,' said Nessie through a large smile, 'where the people think that we're all the same plesiosaur and we're all called Nessie. As if! Where there's one, there are always two! It's where I got my name from,' she said proudly. 'Loch Ness - in the Highlands.'

Brodie's brain nearly burst through his skull under the sudden surge of excitement. 'You mean - where those bare-skinned animals live?' He tripled around the cavern in nervous excitement.

'Why yes. Looks like some of your ancestors just couldn't keep a good secret down. Now who's coming to Loch Ness with me - better hurry whilst we've still got a clear night.'

'Why do you only go when the sky is shining with colours?'

'You mean the Aurora Borealis ... the Northern Lights? They're such a beautiful sight that anybody who sees them is compelled to remain still for hours just staring at them. So, they forget about us. I like to watch them too, and go through for a change and a bit of mischief,' she said with a twinkle in her oversized eye. 'But, that's only our cover for the winter. We do sometimes go through in summer, but it's more dangerous then.'

Brodie watched the large plesiosaurs mumble amongst themselves and roll around in the water. They were so large. To him, it looked like the world was revolving. 'Can I come?' he said suddenly.

The mumbling ceased immediately and they turned back in the water and stared at him once again. Brodie felt mildly uncomfortable at the wall of massive eyes.

'Err … I said, can I come?'

'Impossible.'

'Why?'

Nessie bowed her head and debated about saying any more. She took a deep, steadying breath before responding. 'Because our ancestors brought you here for good. The white witch, Noremac, cleared the Highlands of all haggises to protect them from the black witch, Gertruda McNorris. This will be your only home … although … some of your type did take a wrong turn and we lost them down the red tunnel.'

'Red tunnel?' asked Brodie.

'Yes - down there.'

Brodie looked through the water and for the first time

noticed that the rainbow-coloured light was actually coming out of seven separate tunnels just below the surface of the water, each with a different colour - red, orange, yellow, green, blue, violet and indigo.

'So where does the red one go?'

'A place where it's so hot that the mud bubbles and hot water gushes out of the ground. We don't go there often. Anyway - Charles - you take this inquisitive, furry beastie back to Darmaeddie Loch. I'm taking Petula to Loch Ness. Come Petula. And Brodie,' Nessie said with an air of concern in her voice.

'Yes?'

Her eyes narrowed. 'Make sure you go home over land. You were very lucky to get free from the kelpie tonight. He won't be happy about that and certainly won't let it happen twice.'

'But the storm.'

'The storm will have died down now. It'll take you a great deal longer, but at least you'll get home that way. Don't ever try coming back here and be sure not to tell anyone else about us.'

Nessie lowered her head so that her scaly nose was close to Brodie.

'Or, we'll have to eat you instead!'

Brodie blinked sharply as she snapped her large, grey teeth at him and he jumped back into the water. He was just a dot compared to the plesiosaurs. Nessie snorted a laugh and she and Petula snaked their way through the other plesiosaurs and headed for the tunnel where the spangled green light was coming from.

'This way for you, Brodie,' gruffed Charles as he swam in the opposite direction. 'Stay close.'

All too quickly Brodie sensed his world falling apart. He felt an enormous tug in his chest as Nessie swam away from him. He was so overwhelmed by compulsion to follow Nessie and Petula as they entered the green tunnel, and in a split second decision, or whether it was a decision Brodie will never know, he swam after them instead of Charles and nipped in close by their fins, careful not to be swiped by them.

Charles continued to swim in the opposite direction as he muttered disapprovingly, unaware of Brodie's escape.

A strange, warm glow washed over Brodie when he swam into the green light with the plesiosaurs. They seemed to glide effortlessly through the water as he paddled furiously to keep up with them. Then everything suddenly rushed past his face with such force that his fur and skin were pulled backwards as he was catapulted through the water into the unknown.

CHAPTER EIGHT

Return to the Highlands

Brodie squeezed his eyes tightly to ease the pounding in his head. He would never be able to explain it, but he had the strangest feeling of loneliness he'd ever experienced as he unpeeled his dry tongue from the roof of his mouth and tried opening his eyes, but they were welded shut. His throat and chest felt like they were being scraped with sandpaper and nails through every breath he took. As consciousness slowly seeped back into his heavy, aching body, he remembered Nessie calling out to him.

'You shouldn't have come Brodie. Stay low until the next Aurora Borealis - we'll come for you ... if it's safe. Take care, little one.'

Brodie remembered Nessie slipping away from him as he was pulled in the opposite direction. Pulled by what, he couldn't remember - but it was strong. A cool, crisp wind blew across his already cold body. He shivered. His insides ached with hunger. Despite many attempts to move, his limbs remained numb and motionless. He wasn't really sure if he was dead or alive or even where he was.

Freezing cold water bit into him as it lapped around his head and shoulders. He must be on the shore he thought, finally managing to prise open his eyes. It was daylight, or greylight, as the sky was very dull and dank. It had been so clear last night. He remembered seeing green and red pulses in the star-speckled sky, although only briefly before he blacked out. Through waterlogged ears, he could hear muffled cawing sounds from the birds flying in the sky above him. He tried moving again, but his muscles remained defiant to his wishes.

The sound of feet crunching on the pebbly shore disturbed

his thoughts. He froze and shut his eyes as the footsteps grew nearer until they stopped right beside him. Brodie's heart was beating so hard that he thought whatever was beside him must be hearing it. His bowels loosened like they would if a midge was about to bite him - well, he thought, at least something else was moving.

There was a long and painful silence, apart from the black birds cawing.

A shadow moved over him.

He kept his eyes shut.

The shadow moved again.

Brodie felt defenceless. Nothing was moving. He couldn't run or scream. After a few more seconds, he could bear the suspense no longer and flicked open his leathery eyelids. A loud, blood-curdling scream escaped from his mouth and his nail-lined throat, that wouldn't allow him to utter a simple word just a few moments ago, vibrated and rattled until he ran out of breath.

Erin's voice pierced the still morning as she screamed back at him even louder. When she first saw the clump of ginger-red fur lying on the pebbles she thought some unfortunate child had lost its toy, or that it was a wig. But on closer inspection and with the foul smell coming from it, she assumed that it was a dead animal washed up from the loch.

Brodie drew breath to scream again and only then realised that the porcelain-white face leaning over him was screaming even louder than he was. Energy flooded back into his body. He bolted upright and drew his face closer to the strange creature, fixing it with his penetrating, light blue stare as he cocked his head to one side and then to the other and examined its face carefully.

Erin mirrored him as they sat in silence and stared curiously at one another.

'You know,' said the young girl calmly stretching her hand out to Brodie, 'you're the strangest creature I've ever seen in my whole life.'

Brodie managed to clamber to his feet and moved back towards the water. He felt a bit unsteady as he regained the feeling in his legs.

Erin snatched her hand back like she had burnt it and retreated a few steps. They both remained silent, cautiously sweeping their eyes over one another.

He was the size of a small cat.

She was the size of a … well, Brodie didn't know because he'd never seen anything walking on two legs apart from the birds. And the kelpie. She was probably the size of the kelpie. A cruel knot suddenly formed in Brodie's stomach. KELPIE?

Erin's red, curly hair hung from beneath an aqua-green hat and draped itself around her delicate shaped face. Her mouth and nose were blood-red against the chilly morning. She zipped her black fleece up to her neck and adjusted her hat. Her red eyebrows knitted together in concern as she stared widely at Brodie's three, leathery legs and his strange feet.

'You poor thing, you've hurt yourself,' she said moving towards him. 'You've lost a leg.'

Brodie stared crossly at her. 'And you've lost your mind. These are all the legs I'm supposed to have. What happened to your face - you've no fur on it? You're a kelpie, aren't you? Leave me alone!' He took a few more steps back.

Erin's mouth hung open as she stared at Brodie in utter disbelief. Her blue eyes widened innocently. 'You talk?'

'Course I do, stupid. Never met anyone who doesn't. The birds, the rabbits, the Monarch of the Glen, even the fish. Oh - and Nessie.'

Erin gasped and pinched herself. It hurt, so she wasn't dreaming. She squinted her eyes at Brodie and then blinked widely to clear them. He was still standing there - he wasn't a figment of her imagination either.

'Don't tell me. You think I'm ugly too? Well, the feeling's mutual! Strange bunch of animals,' Brodie muttered as he paced the shore and kicked at the pebbles. He stubbed one of his toes and hopped around on one leg cradling the sore toe with his other hand … or was it his foot. 'Ouch! Ooh! Ouch. You'd think they hadn't seen a haggis before,' he muttered miserably, his toe throbbing painfully.

Erin giggled.

Then something inside Brodie clicked and he froze to the spot as he realised the significance of a furless face. Slowly and cautiously, he turned back towards Erin and stared pointedly at her.

Erin's smile faded and she returned the stare as she gazed at Brodie's three legs, his ginger-red fur, his strange shape.

Their eyes widened knowingly and they yelled together.

'HAGGIS?'

'PEOPLE?'

The birds squawked loudly overhead.

'Erin? Erin? Are you ok?' Erin's mother rushed out of the trees like she'd been fired out of a cannon after she'd heard the screaming.

'Quick, you funny animal … thing. I'll hide you in here. You'll be safe, for now, but you must hide!' Erin unwrapped the aqua-green scarf from her neck and spread it across the pebbles.

Brodie flicked his eyes around worriedly as he surveyed the unfamiliar surroundings. Where would he be safer? He looked back. The mist was lying low over the loch and added an air of mystery to its intense beauty. But something had happened out there last night that he couldn't remember and it frightened him too much to go back into the water. He looked at Erin beckoning him to hide.

'Erin honey - are you ok?' A tall, slim woman with a

cream, Arran hat pulled down over her strawberry-blonde hair stumbled from the trees and rushed over to Erin, pausing briefly to examine her cream corduroy jeans. 'Dash, I knew it was too wet to wear this colour today,' she sighed as she rubbed at some dirt with her leather-gloved hand.

Brodie darted across the pebbles and launched himself onto the scarf, although he didn't know how standing on it would make him invisible.

Erin threw the scarf over his head and just managed to wrap him up before her mother was at her side. Brodie was helpless. He had no idea what to expect next.

'I thought I heard you scream?' asked Erin's mother, pursing her mulberry painted lips as she folded her arms and rubbed her hands on them to generate some warmth against the cold morning.

Erin bundled her scarf inside her fleece. 'No - wasn't me.' A small whimper escaped Brodie's lips as Erin unwittingly poked her finger in his eye.

'What?' asked Brenda looking around like she'd lost something.

Erin craned her neck and watched the black birds circling above her. She nodded to her mother. 'Must be them you're hearing Mum.'

Brenda squinted her mascara-lined eyes at the birds and nodded. 'Maybe - strange though. Anyway - another haul of pebbles I suppose?'

'Huh?'

Brenda pointed to her daughter's bulging jacket.

'Yes - just a few to polish up.'

Pangs of hunger stabbed at Brodie's stomach as it rumbled loudly.

'And, by the sound of your stomach, you need doorstep

slices of toast for your breakfast. Come on or you'll be late for school.' Brenda sniffed at the air. 'There's the most awful smell around here too,' she muttered and disappeared back into the clump of trees just as it began to snow heavily. Erin followed on behind her mother as they wound their way along the trodden path towards the house.

The black birds continued to circle the sky above them, cawing loudly.

The white painted gate at the bottom of the garden creaked loudly as Erin pushed it shut with her foot. The snow had covered the garden completely, but she could still see indentations in the snow where the stepping-stones extended peacefully along the lawn to the back of the house. Her father didn't like anyone walking on the lawn in such damp weather so she was careful to make sure that she stepped on the stones. Once at the back door, she kicked off her boots, ran through the kitchen and up the stairs to her bedroom without taking off her jacket.

'Erin - come back here with those pebbles!' Brenda shook her head dismissively. She'd never understand ten-year olds.

Safely shut in the warmth of her bedroom, Erin unzipped her fleece and carefully tipped Brodie out onto the bed. Although he was glad to stretch himself out again, Erin's body had the warmth of his mother's embrace and he had felt somewhat at ease. She wasn't going to be a danger to him he thought as he watched her rushing around the room picking things up from one place and putting them back down again in another place.

There was a loud knock at the door.

Brodie took a sharp intake of breath, his eyes widened with terror and he somersaulted backwards off the bed, landing hard on the carpeted floor.

'Quick - get under here,' said Erin lifting the valance sheet and pushing Brodie towards the bed. Feeling bruised and tired,

Brodie managed to scrabble under the bed where he nursed an injured leg.

'Erin, love.' Brenda opened the door and popped her head around it. 'The school's just phoned. The heating system is on the blink, so you won't have to go back to school until they manage to fix it. Normal lessons will resume on Monday - they hope.'

A broad grin divided Erin's face.

'Well, I can see you're happy with that news. I'll do as much work from home as I can. Remember, your father was on late shift last night so you'll need to keep quiet for most of the day to let him sleep. I may have to go into work for a short time, so I'll either leave you with Rose Stewart or drop you at the Nessie Exhibition Centre so you can help your Aunty whilst I'm gone.'

Erin groaned painfully. 'If I must do any, I'd rather do the latter Mum. You can't leave me with Mrs Stewart and that horrible son of hers. Please don't do that to me.'

Brodie listened to the clear, female voices as they chattered away for a few minutes. They were different to anything he'd heard before. Soothing too. After the door closed, he heard Erin scuffle around the room and tried to follow the noise with his eyes. Then everything went quiet. He held his breath as he strained to listen to any movement - there was nothing. Then he shrieked and hit his head off the bottom of the bed when Erin's face suddenly appeared in front of him, upside down.

Erin lay on her stomach and hung over the end of the bed as she stared at Brodie. 'Right, you strange creature - come out now and tell me who and what you are. I've got to be dreaming - no animal talks, or looks so strange.' She let the green valance sheet drop to the floor and padded across the bedroom carpet and began searching for something.

Brodie rubbed his head and hesitated before rolling out from under the bed. He looked around the large room at the four green walls, then ran his eyes over shelves containing books, games, stuffed toys, a computer, CD player, DVD and television. All things that were completely alien to him. All things that were of no interest or value to him.

Hunger gnawed at his stomach and he sniffed the air for some food. Erin was on her knees, head first inside a cupboard rummaging around and didn't seem to notice Brodie tiptoeing across the opposite side of the bedroom from her. He sidled up to a large, brown animal sitting on the floor with its back resting against the wall.

'How long's she kept you holed up here for?' he whispered, glancing quickly over at Erin to make sure she hadn't heard him.

The large animal remained silent and continued to stare blankly into space.

Brodie felt concern for the animal. 'That bad eh? Look, we can try and escape together. Are you as hungry as I am?' He surveyed its large frame. 'Maybe not - she seems to have fed you well.'

The animal remained motionless.

Brodie became irritated by its ignorance. 'What's wrong? Kelpie got your tongue or something?' His patience snapped and he head butted the bear that Grandmother Scott had given to Erin when she was four. It toppled onto the bedside table, sending the lamp and the alarm clock crashing to the floor. The bells on the clock started to ring loudly. Brodie screeched and rolled over on the floor, plugging his ears with fingers from two of his feet whilst the other leg and foot peddled furiously in the air.

'Sssshhh - do you want to get found out?' Erin plucked herself from the cupboard, rushed over to the alarm clock and pulled the small lever back to stop the ringing. She righted the bedside table, replaced the clock and the lamp and laughed warmly at Brodie. He was still peddling furiously in the air and his face was screwed up so tightly that his eyes had disappeared and all she could see was his fluted nose and four nostrils. She bent down and jabbed him in the side.

Brodie immediately kicked out with all three legs, jumped to his feet and stood to attention, surveying Erin with intent. She was tall, to him. What did she want with him? But his defences waned when she smiled back at him and spoke softly.

'Don't worry, I'm not going to hurt you.' Erin leant towards Brodie, scooped him off the floor and set him on the bed. He'd never felt such softness or such luxury as he snuggled into the duvet. It was how he imagined what sitting on a cloud would feel like.

Erin sat down on the bed next to him and leafed through a small book, pausing for some time over one particular page. She looked at Brodie and then back to the picture, frowned, shook her head in denial, scratched at her brow and then looked at Brodie again.

'You really are, aren't you?'

'What?' said Brodie innocently.

'A h-haggis?' Erin pointed at the picture of a furry creature with three legs. 'OK, it's not exactly like you - maybe not as ugly … or strange - but it's similar.'

Brodie leant over the book and looked down his fluted nose at the picture. He'd never seen a book before, never seen pictures either. His crystal-blue eyes blinked widely as he surveyed the picture, but it meant nothing to him. He was hungry.

Erin noticed the rowan plait around his leathery ankle and reached out to touch it, but Brodie leapt off the bed and ran over to the corner like a wounded animal. He stared challengingly at Erin, unsure of her intentions. His stomach growled loudly.

'Stay right where you are,' Erin said before leaving the room.

*

Brodie stood and drooled over the delicious banquet that unfolded on the bed in front of his gluttonous eyes. It was like Aladdin's cave - only full of a kaleidoscope of rich, colourful food instead of jewels. He had never tasted food like it. Erin explained what each thing was before he ate it, an orange, apple, yoghurt, toast and Walker's chocolate-chip shortbread, but apart from some of the fruit, most of it meant nothing to him. He was too hungry to care and besides, it tasted good which was all he needed to know. He took two bites to eat the unpeeled orange and Erin watched it slide down his short, thick throat. He took an immediate liking to the shortbread and devoured every biscuit, and was about to bite into the crinkly stuff when Erin told him that he couldn't eat the wrapping - whatever that was. But there was plenty of other food and drink for him. After he'd stuffed himself to the brim, he belched his way through an explanation of who he was and how he'd come to be in Loch Ness.

'So, I've no idea what pulled me across the loch,' he said, his stomach gurgling pleasurably as he sat on the bed like a beached whale. 'My father will be furious with me and will make me eat insects. He'll probably be thrown off the Council. I don't even know if I want to go back. And I can only get back if Nessie surfaces.' His eyes drooped dolefully when he thought about what he'd done and how worried, or angry, everyone would be. But, in spite of everything that had happened and regardless of where he was, he now felt pretty good. After a few pensive moments, his eyelids rolled down over his eyes and he slipped into a deep and disturbing sleep.

Erin watched him sleep for some time as she pondered over the haggis. She thought she knew everything there was to know about the mythical creature, but now she wasn't so sure. Maybe the haggis was real and maybe it had returned to the Highlands. Erin moved over to the desk and logged the computer onto the Internet. After typing the word 'haggis' in the search box she sat back in her chair and steepled her fingers against one another as the Google search engine came back with well over one million hits. It was going to be a long research.

*

'Mum - am I coming down with something?' said Erin brushing the curls back from her forehead as she walked into her mother's office that led off the downstairs hall. The office was lined with shelves and shelves of books and folders. At the far end, a small window briefly interrupted the rows of books and looked out onto the snowy, front garden. Brenda waved her hand and signalled to Erin that she'd be finished her phone call in just a few moments.

Erin crossed the room and gazed out of the window as she ran her finger along the spines of some of the books. She'd grown bored of the Internet after the first twenty-five articles repeated much of the same thing. There was nothing new, which hadn't really surprised her. Brenda shuffled papers around the desk as she chatted on the phone. She looked up and smiled at Erin then turned back to her desk and scribbled something down before hanging up the phone.

'Are you feeling ill?' She beckoned Erin over and pressed the palm of her hand against her pale forehead. 'No temperature there.'

Erin frowned. She had to be feeling ill. Nothing else could explain why she thought she was talking to a haggis in her bedroom and even worse, that he had come here with Nessie - the mythical

Loch Ness monster. The only way to confirm it would be to take her mother up to her room and show her. But show her what? If she *was* imagining things, she'd be taken to see a therapist. If she wasn't imagining things, then Brodie would be in danger of being discovered. Discovered - geezo, what was she talking about? Haggises simply didn't exist - apart from a synthetic recipe of offal and oats that people went mad eating every January when they celebrated Robert Burns' birthday.

'You have been acting a bit strange. Maybe you caught a chill down at the loch this morning. Come on, I'll make you a mug of hot chocolate,' Brenda said gently and she got up out of her brown leather chair and left the office. Erin followed her, feeling slightly relieved. At least she hadn't imagined going to the loch.

She climbed up onto the wooden stool at the breakfast bar and watched the mug rotate on the glass plate, only snapping out of her trance when the microwave beeped loudly. Brenda set the mug in front of Erin and pushed a plate of shortbread under her nose before she went back to the office and buried herself in her work. The phone rang for the umpteenth time that morning and Brenda pushed the door of her office shut.

Erin sipped the warm chocolate and nibbled on the shortbread. She simply didn't believe in ghosts, witches, pixies or the Loch Ness monster. Or anything else like that. She was far too logical and grown up for her ten years and was never one to be frightened by ghostly stories.

"You see want you want to believe," was always her response. "I don't believe, so I'll never see a ghost or any other mythical legend. It's just pure nonsense." Then it struck her like a bolt of lightening. Maybe she was beginning to believe! She looked up at the ceiling. The sound of deep snoring was coming from upstairs. It wasn't her father - he didn't snore that loudly. It was coming from her room. She slammed her mug on the breakfast bar, launched herself off the stool, scooted out of the kitchen and scaled the stairs two at a time.

CHAPTER NINE

Haggis Hunting Season

Brodie peered through the white, swirling mist trying to focus on the blurry figure beyond. As it moved towards him - slowly - it grew darker, blacker and less blurry, but the mist continued to mask its true identity. He strained to listen to what it was saying to him through the sound of his own heart pounding in his ears as sweat prickled at his skin. The hazy figure kept moving towards him. An outline of a face came into view. He wanted to turn and run, but his feet seemed to be glued to the ground. He looked down to see what was holding them, but all he could see was mist. He couldn't move, no matter how hard he tried; he was stuck. He yelled.

A blinding white light flashed in front of him and the dark figure quickly retreated. The mist started to clear and a white figure stood in front of him, smiling - he thought - but he couldn't be sure through the swirling mist.

Brodie stirred from his sleep and flicked his eyes open to darkness. It was just a dream. A bad one at that. A feint light trickled into the darkness through a small mesh just above him as he swayed gently back and forth. His stomach gurgled.

'Good morning Erin, no school today?' asked Mrs Robertson in her usual, syrupy tones. 'And how's your Mum and Dad?'

'The heating's broken down, so we've no school until Monday at the earliest. Mum and Dad are fine, thanks - I'll tell them you were asking, Mrs Robertson,' said Erin hurriedly. Brodie listened to the different voices that spoke to Erin as they asked her the same questions and Erin replied politely, but hurriedly to them. He wriggled himself around so that he could see out through the small mesh panel and admired the tartan scarf on the white-haired women who had just spoken to Erin.

'Good morning Erin!' bellowed Mr Gunn through his deep, crusty voice as he walked towards his white van. His four, hairless chins were folded on top of one another like a roman blind and they wobbled like jelly when he spoke. He was a ruddy-faced, plump man and displayed a gold filling on his front tooth when he smiled. A greying moustache dressed his beetroot-red mouth and his green eyes sparkled with mischief. He was wearing a white, stained apron that was straining under the weight of his belly and the white cap he was wearing hid the fact that he had very little hair.

'Good morning Mr Gunn,' said Erin, 'a nice, crisp morning.'

'Aye, it is that. After the clear night last night - I was surprised at the snow this morning. Weather forecast says we're in for a real dump of snow over the next few days. What are you up to this early then? Shouldn't you be thinking about going to school?' He looked at Erin through squinted eyes and rubbed chin number one with his large, shovel-sized hand.

Erin smiled graciously and explained that the heating had broken down. Mr Gunn shook his head and laughed heartily as he brushed snow from her hat.

'Thought you kids of today would still be tucked up in bed watching your fancy portable TVs or playing computer games. Well, tell your mother I'm just about to go out into the hills and shoot some more haggis for her. They're easier to find in the snow, you know. But, they're mighty nimble on those three legs. This old fat body,' he said placing his hands over his large stomach, 'isn't quite as nimble as it used to be. I've got a good shot though, so I'm sure I'll have enough haggis for the Robert Burns' celebrity bash your mother's arranged for tomorrow night. Any clues at who's going to be there?'

Erin's cold lips forced a smile as she worried about Brodie

in her rucksack. The only way she had seemed able to stop him from snoring was to either keep prodding him or keep him moving so she had eased him into the rucksack and gone out for a walk around the village. Once a haggis was in a deep sleep, virtually nothing could wake it.

'No, I don't know who's going to be there,' said Erin, although she had heard her mother speaking to some agents about who would be there but had been sworn to secrecy to protect them from the media. 'In fact - what makes you think it's even a celebrity bash?'

Mr Gunn curled his mouth into a faint smirk. 'Oh come on Erin - I'm a wee bit brighter than that. All this fuss? No tickets to buy for it and all this hush, hush? It has to be for celebrities. I heard there are some real important A-list celebrities flying in from America tomorrow. Might catch a glimpse of them when I'm delivering the haggis to the castle. Oops, better go back and get my haggis shot gun,' he said mischievously, his eyes almost disappearing into his flabby skin as he grinned. He burst into a deep, menacing laughter. 'Tasty little beasts.'

Brodie gulped slowly and a knot formed in his stomach when he saw Mr Gunn's narrowed eyes. They seemed to be staring right at him through the fine mesh.

'And I'm a bit brighter than that, Mr Gunn! Everybody knows that haggises are just a myth. I mean, I know the recipe,' said Erin boldly. Her breath curled from her mouth against the cold morning.

'Ach Erin, you're too grown up for your own good, child. I only use the recipe if I can't find a real haggis - you know that.' His eyes twinkled and his gold tooth shone brightly against his grey teeth when he grinned. 'But I don't have to cheat often - I'm usually pretty successful, especially this time of year. It's haggis hunting season and it usually doesn't take long before the stupid beasties are running after me when I start playing the old bagpipes.' He patted Erin gently on the back and pulled at her rucksack before saluting her and getting into his van.

Erin rolled her blue eyes and continued to walk briskly up the road. 'Aye, whatever you say Mr Gunn. Whatever you say.'

'Erin? D-d-did he really mean that?'

Erin coughed nervously. 'He's just making it up, Brodie. Believe me, nobody in the world believes that the haggis is a real living animal. Not even me - I just believe I'm going mad!'

The park was deserted when Erin arrived - no children running around, nobody walking their dogs - just pure silence. Not even footprints. The snow was fresh. But, it was still early enough in the morning for visitors. And it was bitterly cold. She strode to the centre of the park so that she would have time to get Brodie back in the rucksack before anyone got close to them. A quick glance over her shoulder confirmed that there was nobody else around so she set the bag down on the snowy ground and tipped it onto its side.

'Ok, Brodie. Time to get out and make a snowman. I need to think about what I'm going to do with you and how you're going to get back to where you came from. That's easy - it's all in my mind, so I just need to reformat it like a computer disk and programme it with something else. Maybe a programme to make me believe that Daniel Radcliffe has asked me out on a date - now that would be cool.'

Brodie tumbled from the rucksack and yawned widely. He had never felt so tired before. 'When I went in search of the truth behind the myths and legends, I didn't think I'd really find anything. But I have - or maybe I'm dreaming. Nobody believed me back at home, and now you don't believe me here. Why do I seem to be the only one to believe anything?' A tinge of sadness filled Brodie's face as he fought against his feelings. His bagpipe wails echoed around the park.

Erin slapped her pale forehead with her gloved hand. 'Just when I thought I was blanking my mind of haggises and now I've got one that cries,' she muttered. 'OK, OK - I believe you! Now get a grip of yourself and stop that crying or we'll have the entire village complaining about the noise. I need time to think - so stay close.'

Brodie stopped crying and blinked widely at Erin as she rolled snow into two different sized balls and stacked the smaller one on top of the larger one. He tripled around after her and watched in silence as she pulled a carrot, and two pieces of coal from the side pocket of her rucksack. She pushed the carrot into the front of the smaller snowball for the nose, pressed the coal into the snow for eyes and then ran her index finger through the snow beneath the carrot drawing in a mouth. She then carefully moulded some snow onto the body to form arms.

'Wow,' said Brodie coolly, 'so that's what a snowman is?'

Erin nodded silently as she tied her scarf around the snowman's neck and set her hat on top of its head. The northerly breeze swirled the snowflakes around the snowman making it look like a scene from a Christmas card.

A dog's feisty barks broke the silence of the morning. Erin shot around and looked back towards the village. Mr Stewart was heading towards them with Rusty.

Erin pointed across the park. 'Quick, back in the bag – Mr Stewart's walking his dog.' Brodie's heart lurched and he pivoted his head around to see a man in the distance approaching with something on four legs.

'Dog?'

'Yes, you know - four legs, a tail and it barks?'

'Barks? As on a tree? Strange concept. Never seen one,' said Brodie curiously as he sucked on some snow.

'Shut up and get in the bag. If anyone finds out what you are - you'll be taken from me and they'll do all these experiments on you and put you in a cage and all these people will stare at you and they'll maybe clone you and then try and breed you and then farm you ...'

Brodie had heard enough. He dived headfirst into the black rucksack and trembled with fear. He once thought that the cold stares of Uisdean McGillis were something to fear. That was nothing compared to how he felt now. The louder the dog's barking grew, the more Brodie trembled.

'Stop moving around in there and keep very quiet.' Erin pulled the ties at the neck of the bag together tightly and lifted it onto her back just as Rusty bounded up to her, growling and barking hungrily. Her stomach lurched when she noticed Brodie's unusual footprints in the snow and quickly started walking over them before Mr Stewart arrived.

'Considering the school is closed, you're on the go early this morning lass,' said Mr Stewart. 'William's still unconscious in his bed.' Mr Stewart was a tall, well-built man with dirty-blonde hair and a matching dirty-blonde moustache on an aging, but placid, face. His cheeks and nose were bright red from the cold air and his brown eyes sparkled with winter freshness. His dog, Rusty, was a medium-sized Heinz 57 variety with rough, short fur and was as annoying as Mr Stewart's son. He had already taken a keen interest in the contents of Erin's rucksack as she continued to mask Brodie's footprints with her own.

'Y-yes, Mr Stewart … nothing like being up with the birds,' she said sheepishly, continuing to walk in circles around the snowman.

Brodie's teeth chattered as he trembled. The dog's ears pricked up slightly and he cocked his head to one side to listen. Then he barked even louder and jumped up at the rucksack, biting into the bottom of it.

Brodie muffled a scream.

'Rusty! Get away from there you menace.' Mr Stewart pushed the aggressive dog away with his foot, but Rusty barked continuously and kept going back to the bag.

Erin apologised and forced a smile. 'It's ok Mr Stewart - you know me and him don't seem to get on. I was just going anyway.'

Mr Stewart nodded. 'You've been busy. I do like the snowman. Oh, but they're strange footprints indeed.'

Erin cringed. She hadn't managed to cover all of Brodie's footprints and hoped Mr Stewart wouldn't notice. But no, not Mr Stewart. He bent down and mulled them over carefully.

'Very strange indeed,' he mused.

'Footprints? Oooh, I never noticed them. So they are,' said Erin rather feebly as she pretended to mull them over with her neighbour. She wondered if he would detect her cover-up. Mr Stewart had taken early retirement from the police force the year before, but he never ceased to find suspicion with anything just slightly out of the ordinary and would nearly always start to examine the truth that really lay behind it. Even if it was glaringly obvious.

'Hmm … wonder what on earth they could be? And, they are only around here. Look - your footprints are the only other ones in the park, apart from old Rusty's there and mine. That is, apart from these ones around the snowman. They look fresh too.'

Erin forced a smile. 'Maybe it's some sort of bird? Anyway - must go. I'll leave it to the expert to sort out,' she said with urgency, still moving around to keep Rusty from biting the rucksack.

'This belong to you then?'

Erin's heart stopped momentarily and she squeezed her eyes tightly together, hesitating before turning around to look at

Mr Stewart. Relieved and smiling gratefully, she ran back to untie her scarf from the snowman's neck. 'Bye!' she chirped, snatched her hat from the snowman's head and marched briskly away from Mr Stewart. Rusty followed her, barking and growling at the rucksack. But there was really nothing new in Rusty's antics towards Erin, so she continued to ignore him as if nothing was wrong.

'See you tonight, Erin,' said Mr Stewart. 'Rusty! Rusty! Come back here now.'

Erin raised her arm and waved back to Mr Stewart. 'Yes, see you tonight.' She sighed heavily. That's the last thing she needed right now - an evening with his darling son William.

Brodie's nerves trembled like jelly. He was beginning to feel a bit like a hunted haggis. 'I take it then,' he said from the depths of the rucksack, 'that dogs are dangerous?'

Erin didn't answer. She just kept on walking to gain as much distance between them and Rusty.

CHAPTER TEN

The Dryads

Erin had a strange feeling that she was being watched. Ever since she had been at the loch earlier on that morning. A shiver ran down her spine and the hairs on the back of her neck prickled. Black birds began circling the sky above her, cawing loudly as she crunched her way through the snowy park. It was almost like they were following her.

SPLAT!

A white lump of bird pooh landed on the arm of her jacket.

SPLAT!

Another landed on her rucksack. Then one bird swooped down over Erin. It was a raven. She shrieked loudly and ducked as another swooped down at her. One after the other the ravens dive-bombed her and if she wasn't ducking out of their way she was sidestepping a continual splatter of raven pooh. She ran around in a panicked frenzy.

Brodie was tossed around inside the rucksack like a pancake. Struggling to stay on his feet, he caught a glimpse of what was happening through the fine mesh and he squealed with fear. He spied the rowan trees across two fields. 'Run for the trees, Erin. They're rowan - they'll protect us. Run fast!'

Birds lived in trees so Erin wasn't sure how the trees would protect them. There weren't any leaves, so they wouldn't provide much cover either. But through lack of choice for a better option, she obeyed Brodie and sprinted through the snow, nearly losing her footing a few times as she scrambled over a snow-covered flagstone wall and made a mad dash across the field for cover. Brodie fell over again and bounced continually off the bottom of the bag as Erin ran on. Once in the small thicket of rowan trees, the ravens circled in the sky above cawing loudly, but strangely enough they didn't perch in any of the trees or come into the forest.

Brodie untangled his legs and stood up again. 'Told you they'd protect us,' he said feeling smugly relieved as he surveyed the many rowan tree trunks. It was all he could see from the rucksack.

Erin slid the rucksack from her shoulders, set it on the snow-covered forest floor and helped Brodie out. His crystal-blue eyes grew dark and serious and his breathing became rapid and shallow as he looked around himself.

'What's wrong?'

'We're in a forest!'

'Duh - you did tell me to.'

'I thought they were just a few rowan trees, but there's a forest of them and it's so dark in there,' he said nodding towards the fir trees. 'We aren't allowed in forests. It's dangerous for us.' He looked up through the wintry branches at the birds still circling the snowy sky.

'Why is it dangerous for you?'

'I don't know - we're just told not to go in them.'

Erin was puzzled and took on a motherly tone as she spoke to Brodie. 'Don't worry - you're with me. We're not going into the dark forest - I only go in there with my Dad. And besides - you said the rowan trees would protect you, so,' she said curiously rubbing the light-coloured trunk of the tree nearest to her, 'what's so special about them?'

'Rowan trees are our Silent Protector. Look,' said Brodie stretching out his leg. 'This is rowan wood - I made it to protect me when I left home.' Erin listened intently as Brodie explained about how they believed the rowan trees protected them.

'There is a myth that rowan trees protect us from witches too,' said Erin. 'No other evil - just witches. But it's a myth,

Brodie. The trees can barely protect themselves,' she said rolling her eyes playfully and laughing.

Brodie suddenly jumped around the forest like his feet were on fire. 'So there is a witch then. I knew there was! I knew there was! Nessie talked about one too, but I can't quite remember her name. A white witch too …'

Erin looked on fascinated as Brodie jumped around in excitement. His large eyes rolled around in his head and his mouth flapped continuously as he chattered ten to the dozen about how right he had been to follow his instincts. After a few minutes, Erin finally interrupted him.

'Not so fast Brodie. We have a few legendary witches, but their powers are simply myth. They're nothing more than evil old women spouting a lot of hub-a-bub nonsense to try and scare people. Goodness knows where the myth about the rowan tree came into it, probably from them too.' Erin widened her blue eyes and wiggled her fingers and hands like she was trying to cast a spell on Brodie.

'I'd be careful about not saying that too loudly.'

Brodie and Erin exchanged hurried glances and looked around themselves, their eyes wide and questioning. But they saw nobody.

'Who said that?' they cried in unison.

A short silence followed.

'I did. Up here,' said a soft and child-like voice.

They both craned their necks upwards and scanned the treetops. There was still nothing to see.

'Look harder - you'll see me then.'

They were silent for about a minute. Then Brodie saw something faint move in the treetops. His eyes shone widely and his mouth broke into a satisfied smile. 'Yes, I can see!'

'See what? I can't see anything,' Erin protested.

'Look harder - into the centre. You'll see,' said Brodie

brimming with euphoria.

As Erin squinted hard, one of the trees seemed to come to life. A nymph-like creature with green tinged hair and almost translucent wings emerged from one of its main arteries. Its skin was the same as the bark on the tree. Its ears were like the knots in the tree, and its face was long and pointed. The dryad stared down with its warm, brown eyes and smiled gently at them.

'We love air, so we stay up here,' she said in a melodic, friendly voice. 'Will you sing to us?'

Erin stood aghast and her mouth opened and closed like a fish. She was speechless, but finally managed a croak. 'You're not … you … a dryad?'

Brodie wasn't so fazed by it. He continued to look on with dizzy excitement.

The dryad smiled warmly. 'Of course - and my friends too.' More nimble-looking dryads emerged from the other trees and surveyed Erin and Brodie carefully as if they were aliens.

'It's nice to see a haggis back here again, but you're playing with fire. We don't like fire.'

The other dryads gasped and a whooshing sound, like leaves blowing in the wind, echoed around the treetops. Except there was no wind, and there were no leaves.

Brodie tripled around the trees anxiously and looked from one dryad to the next. 'What do you mean, playing with fire?'

'Well … I'm not supposed to say anything …'

'Say what for crying out loud,' said Erin becoming impatient with the mind game that the dryad was playing.

'Ooh. Temper gets you nowhere! If that's how you want it to be, then I'm not speaking!' said the dryad crossly as she lay back against the branch and began to merge into the tree. The others copied her.

'No, no. She didn't mean it,' said Brodie desperately.

'Don't go. Please?'

The dryad began to fade into the tree, but hesitated. 'Ok, I won't go if you sing for us. Please young haggis, sing for us.'

'You sing too?' Erin asked perplexed as she looked down at the ball of ginger-red fur she'd happened across at the loch just a few hours ago.

Brodie sat down on the forest floor with two of his legs aligned neatly in front of him, blew his nose into the snow and cleared his throat. He rolled his head 360 degrees on his body, smiled at Erin and snapped it back around like it was on a piece of elastic.

'Aw, I hate it when I do that,' he said rocking slightly as he regained his balance. Then he settled down and began to sing.

Erin's skin prickled when the most enchanting of musical sounds emerged from Brodie's mouth and nose, each of his four nostrils opening and closing at different times to produce different notes. There were no words - just music. Erin thought she'd died and gone to heaven. The nearest it could be likened to was a few people playing the bagpipes, a long distance away, combined with a choir of the sweetest angels singing - almost like pan-bag-pipe music. The forest seemed to stand still as Brodie sung on, totally absorbed in his own music. When he finished five minutes later, a muffled applause echoed around the forest - from the trees above and from the ground below. Erin looked about to see who the applause was coming from, but apart from the dryads in the treetops - she could see nothing.

'Ah Brodie. The forest has missed the mystical tones of the haggis. Welcome back.'

Brodie's eyes filled with concern as he looked up at the dryad. 'Why did we leave in the first place? What have you got to tell me that you're not supposed to?'

The dryad slipped down the tree trunk a little, but the others seemed to be warning her off. 'I can't say too much,' she said looking around the forest cautiously before reducing her voice to a whisper. 'All I can tell you is that we knew the haggis wasn't dead - can't be because the witch isn't - dead, that is. You've a lot of friends in the forest - but you also have enemies too. Be careful. We can protect you here - but not in those trees over there.'

'Why haven't I seen any of you in the rowan trees back at home? We call them our Silent Protectors - protecting us from all evil. Look - I've even tied some rowan wood around my ankle to keep me protected when I'm away from them.'

The dryad shook her head sadly. 'My dear, dear haggis. You will not be protected by that. It is not the wood of the rowan that protects you. It's us. And we can only protect you against the witch - nothing else. Our energy is very powerful and is dangerous to a black witch.' The dryad paused briefly and looked around the forest as if someone else may be listening to her.

'We have our own world in the airy treetops and only reveal ourselves when we are needed - when there's danger. You don't need us wherever you stay now. This forest is surrounded by rowan trees so the witch is holed up in there. Beware - she has friends that will do anything for her. The only way she can get out of the forest is if someone, other than from the faerie world, invites her. And nobody ever has, surprise, surprise.' The dryad looked up towards the sky at the black birds. 'Those ravens are hers and they're watching you, and me.'

A whooshing sound ran through the treetops again. 'We are not your Silent Protector - only you will discover what that is. I must go - I've said too much. Be careful young haggis.' The dryads merged back into the trees and were gone. The forest was silent once again, apart from the ravens.

'To see one raven is lucky, but it's certain misfortune to see two ...,' Erin muttered as she looked up at them through the fluttering snow, circling like vultures looking for their next meal.

A twig cracked behind Brodie and Erin and they swung around. There was nothing to be seen amongst the many tree trunks. Erin's mobile phone rang loudly and they both leapt out of their skins.

'Yes Mum?' said Erin after she'd fumbled nervously for a few seconds before she found the phone buried in the lining of her pocket. 'Ok, I'll be home straight away.' Erin looked at her watch. It had stopped. It couldn't be, it was kinetic - it had no battery; worked on motion and would only stop if it didn't sense movement after a few days. She shook her wrist violently. She'd have to ask her father to get it fixed.

Another twig cracked behind them like someone had stepped on it. Brodie darted his eyes around the forest. Was he imagining things moving?

'Can we go now?' he said shivering through fear rather than cold. It stabbed at his stomach like needles, fear unlike no other he'd felt before. He looked at the rowan plait as his confidence drained from him. He was no longer safe - if he ever was in the first place.

CHAPTER ELEVEN

Noremac

Brenda noticed a flicker of concern cross her daughter's pale face as she came through the back door.

'Everything ok Erin?' She looked at the streaks of bird pooh over Erin's jacket and rucksack and rushed to her side.

Erin pulled away from her quickly. 'Y-yes. Everything's fine Mum. Just unfortunate that's all. Don't know why people say bird pooh is lucky,' she joked nervously as she kicked off her boots and slid out of her jacket. Luckily the ravens hadn't followed her home. They had disappeared into the dark forest.

'Let me take your jacket and bag - I'll get them to the cleaners.'

'NO!'

Brenda stood aghast at her daughter's sudden reaction.

Brodie pinned his ears close to his head and squeezed his eyes shut.

Erin apologised. 'Sorry Mum. I'll sponge them down later. I'll just empty the bag in my bedroom first.' She raised her left wrist. 'This new watch that I got for Christmas has stopped. I didn't think it was supposed to unless it didn't sense any movement for a few days.'

Brenda took Erin's small wrist between her manicured hands and examined the watch carefully. 'You must be imagining things dear - its still going.' She checked the time with her own watch. 'Keeping accurate time too, I have to say.'

Erin snatched her wrist from her mother and examined the watch herself. 'But ... oh ... I must've imagined it. One of those days.' Erin sighed and trampled through the kitchen wearily as she headed for her bedroom.

'I have to leave for Inverness in half an hour. Mrs Stewart has agreed to take you this afternoon.'

Erin groaned heavily.

'Not necessary,' said Ralph through a croaky voice as he met Erin on the stairs. 'I can't sleep - maybe something to do with the phone ringing all morning?' He smiled sleepily at his wife.

'Sorry Ralph - but the school's closed today and I couldn't leave Erin on her own. Since you're up, I'll leave now. I've got a heap of organising to do before the dinner tomorrow night.'

The phone rang violently and Brenda dashed across the kitchen to answer it.

'Yes, that's right. I need fifteen cars to go to Skibo Castle tomorrow night to take them to Urquhart Castle. And I need ten cars to go to Dalcross airport and pick up those that are flying in by private jets at the same time yes … that's right. They must be the best cars in Inverness - these people aren't used to horses and carts you know,' Brenda said jokingly, but there was a stern tone in her voice. If Brenda asked for the best, she expected the best.

'Although, I'm sure they probably won't expect more than a horse and cart driven by a tartan-clad man with red hair wearing a tartan tammy on his head.' The stress that had been showing on her face ebbed away as she laughed freely into the phone at her joke. 'Now there's an idea … maybe we can do that next year!' She chatted away and laughed into the phone for a good ten minutes before she ended the call and pushed her hair behind her ears.

'Erin - there'll be a surprise for you tomorrow. Your Harry Potter heart-throb, Daniel Radcliffe, has finally confirmed that he'll be there.'

Erin almost fainted with shock. She'd only made a wish earlier on that morning about him - it was impossible that a wish could come true - especially one so far fetched. Mind you, just because he was going to be in the same room as her, didn't mean that she'd end up in a passionate kiss with him. Her body tingled at the thought and she blushed girlishly, hoping her mother couldn't read her thoughts.

'Ralph, you'll love this one - your sexy Canadian singer, Dion Cameron, is at Skibo Castle now, along with a whole host of other celebs. Madonna and Ant and Dec fly in tomorrow night and there are a few good movie and business moguls too. My lips are sealed - you'll learn more tomorrow night. Don't say anything about those I've just named. Now I must hurry before Ritchie McTouey decides I've stood him up and goes home.' Brenda pulled on a long, black coat and black leather gloves, snatched her briefcase and keys off the breakfast bar and dashed through the hallway, pulling the front door firmly closed behind her.

'Dion Cameron,' said Ralph through a stupid grin, his eyes sparkling lustfully. 'I hope your mother sits me across from her at the dinner table so that I can watch her all night.'

'You're gross Dad. You're a married man and what's more, you're my father!' Erin screwed up her face in disgust.

Ralph chuckled freely and ruffled his hand through Erin's red hair. 'So - I'll have to watch you getting all doey-eyed over Daniel Radcliffe.'

Blushing wildly, Erin ran up the last remaining stairs and slammed into her bedroom. Brodie's ears popped as the door slammed. His nose, fingers and toes tingled as the warmth of the house quickly penetrated his frostbitten skin. Never having experienced any of those feelings before, he began to panic.

'My fingers are going to drop off. I can't feel my nose either! And my ears went funny with that loud bang!'

'Don't be stupid - they've just gone numb with the extreme change in temperature. And I slammed the door - you'll get used to that.'

Brodie looked mystifyingly at Erin and shook his head.

He'd never understand the language and the ways of people.

'What did all that mean back there in the forest?' he asked biting on his toes to get rid of the tingling.

Erin threw herself on the bed, tucked her arms behind her head and stared up at the white ceiling. 'I'm not sure I understand any of it. I've been in that forest nearly every week of my life and I've never seen dryads, a witch, or anything else mythical. It just doesn't make sense. We have to get you back to where you came from and quick.'

A grateful smile spread across Brodie's face. He was already pining for home, even if he did face the prospect of public humiliation. But he suddenly remembered something and replied with an air of concern in his voice. 'Did I say before … it has to be a clear night when the Northern Lights are dancing in the sky.'

'Fat chance of that over the next few days with the weather forecast. Snow, snow and more snow.'

Brodie's ears went limp and his eyes drooped with sadness.

'Sorry there wee haggis - I didn't mean to upset you,' said Erin quickly as Brodie drooped his head between his shoulders. 'I'm sure everything will be ok.'

A smile replaced Brodie's saddened face and he jumped up on the bed beside Erin to study her with his clear blue eyes. 'What do you suppose the tree spirit meant about me finding out what my Silent Protector really is?'

They both turned their attention to the rowan plait that was tied around Brodie's ankle and stared at it for a very long time.

*

Brodie sat mesmerised at the small television that was tucked under the shelves of books whilst Erin furiously typed away on the keyboard, searching the Internet for any information on haggises and when they were last seen in Scotland. She shook her head, tutted, laughed and rolled her eyes at the numerous different recordings of haggis sightings, but they were all just make-believe. There was no solid evidence that haggises ever really existed. They were just too weird a creature to ever have.

'Quick Brodie - under the bed. Dad's coming up the stairs!'

Brodie rushed around the room in a frenzy before diving headfirst into the green valance sheet, as he would if it was heather, but he cracked his head off one of the bed legs. His painful yelp sounded more like a note from a bagpipe.

Erin stared thoughtfully after Brodie as he disappeared under the bed. Legend had it that the bagpipe was invented to mimic the sounds of the haggis to help flush them out of their burrows. Her thoughts were interrupted by her father's gentle knock. His head appeared around the door.

'Just doing my check to see if you're ok. What are you looking at on the Internet?'

'Don't worry Dad, I haven't joined any chat rooms if that's what you're worried about. I know the hidden dangers. I'm just researching, that's all.'

Ralph hovered at the door for a few seconds and then dawdled over to the computer. 'Researching what? Oh … the haggis?' A devilish smile played around the corners of his freckly mouth. 'Wanting to learn up on it for our celebrities tomorrow night? We can have some fun there.' He leaned over Erin's shoulder and chuckled heartily as he read the story on the screen.

Erin scoffed. 'I don't understand why there's so much fuss made over Robert Burns. I mean, what's the attraction?'

Ralph stood tall and moved his gaze to the window. He had red hair just like Erin's, but his eyes were a greeny-blue. He put his hands in the pockets of his khaki trousers and jingled the loose change he had in there, which always annoyed Erin. 'Why don't you research him on the Internet? He's one of Scotland's greatest bards. And besides - celebrating his life is a great excuse to eat mountains of haggis and clapshot … and have a wee dram of Glenmorangie of course.'

Brodie's stomach retched. Eat haggis? What kind of animals were these people?

After the door clicked shut behind Ralph when he left the bedroom, Brodie crawled out from under the bed, ashen and shaking like a leaf. He groaned miserably.

'Erin - I need to go home. I can't bear all this talk about people eating us. Please help me.' His face was full of sadness and he hunched himself over his feet.

Erin continued to rattle away at the keyboard and ignored him. She'd found a good story.

Brodie felt like going to sleep forever because awake, he just seemed to be in a continual nightmare wherever he turned. His attention switched back to the television and he immediately became entranced with a stunning lady who was singing so beautifully and wearing a long, white dress. The bad dream he had had earlier returned to him. The white image through the mist.

'Noremac.'

The clattering of the keyboard stopped as Erin turned around to face Brodie. 'What?' she said screwing up her face.

'Noremac … white witch …' The more Brodie watched the television, the more he drifted into a trance as his dream became clearer. He could see a face. It was haunting.

'Brodie. Brodie?' Even the snapping of Erin's fingers in front of his eyes didn't break the trance.

His heart raced as the image became clearer and clearer. 'Noremac, Noremac,' he chanted again and again.

Erin looked at the television. 'You mean Dion? It's Dion Cameron.' Brodie didn't respond so she leant across and switched the television off. The screen immediately went black, but Brodie continued to stare at it for a few seconds and then blinked rapidly before passing out into a deep sleep. Erin felt disturbed by his actions. She checked that he was breathing normally and gently pushed him back under the bed, prodding him once in a while to stop him from snoring.

CHAPTER TWELVE

Lucky White Heather and a Missing Dog

The red painted door swung open and Erin followed her parents into the Stewart's heavily decorated house where they were greeted by a slightly broad, and very overpowering, Mrs Stewart who was wearing a tight, pink velvet dress that reminded Erin of a giant marshmallow. Her bottle-blonde hair was swept up into a French roll, revealing a short neck dressed with a very expensive-looking diamond necklace. She always tried too hard to impress. Beneath the screeds of makeup she was a stunning lady and looked much prettier when she was dressed more casually. She smiled widely at them, her glamour-white teeth stained with the same pink lipstick that was heavily applied to her lips, and her rouge painted cheeks puffed up, gently crinkling the skin around her emerald-green eyes.

'Nice to see you all together for a change,' she said stretching out her ring-clad hand to Brenda, then Ralph and then Erin as she shook each of their hands strongly before directing them towards the lounge. She decorated it every year, in time for her Christmas and New Year socialising events, but Erin thought it was always worse than the year before. She reckoned Mrs Stewart spent six months of the year planning her social events and redecorating, and the other six months socialising.

Erin blinked unbelievably at the very Egyptian theme - or was it Bedouin, she couldn't be sure - and prodded her mother's hip with her elbow. Brenda's eyebrow arched at the gaudiness of the room. A large gold-coloured Sphinx statue stood in the centre of the room with an oval of smoked glass balanced on top to form a coffee table. The windows were draped with thick folds of gold, red and mustard coloured chintzy fabric. Heavy gold-flocked wallpaper adorned the walls and fine gold nets were draped over the ceiling pendant and lamps. A hundred or so candles flickered, giving the room a sort of mystical atmosphere.

Brenda and Erin exchanged secret glances before sitting down in one corner of the gold-coloured sofa that wrapped around the lounge and was laden with cushions. Erin definitely felt that she was sitting in a Bedouin tent.

'I designed it myself - what do you think?' asked Mrs Stewart as she paraded smugly around the room, fingering the curtains and puffing up the red and brown chintzy cushions.

'Er ... very different Rose ... very unique,' said Brenda politely.

'Well, I think it's ghastly,' said Mr Stewart through a stiffened smile as he appeared in the doorway sporting a casual shirt and chinos. 'God knows where she gets her ideas from - I just sign the cheques and leave her to it. But, I did draw the line at hiring in a snake charmer! Shame you couldn't make it over at New Year - but better late than never,' he said holding out his hand to Ralph. 'Drinks everyone?'

'Yes, it's amazing where time goes,' said Ralph apologetically as he shook Mr Stewart's hand.

After Erin had recovered from the shock of the room Rusty ran past her, chased closely by William. She never ceased to be bowled over by William's handsome good looks and on first (second, third and fourth!) appearance, would date him over Daniel Radcliffe any day. William pushed his clammy hand into her face and stomped on her foot as he rushed past her in pursuit of Rusty. But that was exactly why she'd never ask him out. He was simply horrid. No wonder Rusty always barked at her - the poor dog probably thought that every ten year old was as nasty as William.

'Leave Rusty alone now, William. Say hello to our guests.'

William's perfect nose formed a crinkled knot and his eyes narrowed as he reluctantly said hello before running back out of the room. Erin thought she saw a hint of shyness behind his brown eyes. Rusty had seen something in the darkness of the garden and stood at the conservatory doors barking furiously.

'OK - outside for you if you can't behave.' Mr Stewart opened the door and Rusty launched himself into the snowy garden barking madly. Erin wished he had let William out instead.

*

Brodie's stomach rumbled loudly as he crawled out from under the bed and looked around for Erin. The house seemed quiet. The note that Erin had left for him crinkled under his feet as he stepped on it. He couldn't read so he didn't even know it was a note. His ear angled towards the window. There, it went again. Like something was hitting the window. Just lightly. Occasionally.

Jumping up onto the window seat, Brodie peered through the gap in the curtain. It was dark outside apart from the light coming from the Stewart's conservatory next door. Erin hadn't been able to leave him anything to eat without her parents questioning why she was taking food to the room. She hadn't been able to get a moment when either parent wasn't in the kitchen. The hunger in Brodie's stomach growled again and his eyes widened with ravenous hunger when he spied the holly bush in the middle of the garden. He breathed the air in strongly through his nose as he tried sucking the smell through the double-glazing.

Brodie pushed against the window but it wouldn't move. He scraped the sides with his talons to try and pull it open, but it still didn't move. Staring at the brass handle, he contemplated its usefulness in opening the window. After a few minutes of consideration, he pulled at the handle with one of his hand-like feet.

Nothing happened so he pulled at it again and this time pressed his other two feet hard against the glass. Still nothing happened. After a few more minutes of debate, he decided to try pushing the handle upwards. Success! Chuckling gleefully, Brodie pushed it up a bit more. The catch released and the window immediately swung open, pulling him outside.

The cold night air bit at him as he dangled from the window by one leg, the other two legs scrabbling furiously to grip the handle. Slowly, slowly, slowly, his fingers slipped down the handle until he found himself falling through the night onto the roof below.

Through a stroke of luck, he landed, without too much pain, on his feet and heaved a sigh of relief. But he wasn't out of danger as he started to slide down the roof like a downhill skier, only on three skis instead of two. His screams were distinctive against the very calm and still night air as he launched himself off the roof and into the garden below. Even though there was no wind, the window suddenly slammed shut. Gnomish laughter echoed around the quiet garden.

Badly winded and bruised, Brodie lay motionless in the snow for some time until he heard a snort next to him through the leylandii hedge. It was followed by a bark. Rusty's bark! Two dark, malice eyes stared at Brodie. The dog barked ferociously and pressed his nose through the hedge. Brodie picked himself up off the snowy lawn and looked back to the house. Erin's window was shut tight.

With every second that followed, more of Rusty's body appeared through the hedge. Brodie turned and hobbled as fast as he could towards the holly bush. Rusty broke free from the hedge and lunged at Brodie, only missing him by the fur on his bottom. Brodie crashed through the holly bush and lay battered and bruised inside the bush's protective shell of thorny leaves. Rusty's pointed teeth rattled like knives being sharpened against each other every time he barked.

Brodie squeezed his eyes shut and huddled into a tight ball. Everything became a blur.

*

Erin saw the relief in her father's tired eyes when Mrs Stewart accepted his apology for turning down the after dinner coffee. 'I've had very little sleep today.' He glanced at Brenda. 'Coffee will only keep me awake tonight and I need all the sleep I can get. My wife has a list of chores for me tomorrow and she needs some help with the Burns Supper.'

'Yes, we all need to get an early night. My turn to apologise now - but we really must get going. Thank you for a lovely evening.' Brenda stood up and made for the door. Erin and Ralph followed her and they said their good nights. It was a welcoming click to Erin as the Stewart's front door closed behind them. She raced down the snowy path, along the road a little and up her own garden path, which Ralph had cleared of snow that afternoon. The front door nearly left its hinges as she flung it open. Erin pulled off her shoes and threw them into the cupboard before scaling the stairs to her bedroom. She closed the door and swept her eyes around the room quickly.

'Brodie - it's only me.'

There was no response.

'Brodie?' she said again, this time slightly louder but no reply came back. Erin threw herself down onto the floor and looked under the bed. He wasn't there. Not even under the pillows. She hauled open the cupboards scanning inside them quickly. Nothing. Panic rose in her chest and she ran out onto the landing.

'Careful there,' said Ralph as he sidestepped his frantic daughter. He paused and studied her troubled eyes. 'You alright?

You seem as though you've lost something.'

'N-n-no Dad,' said Erin, finding it hard to talk without her voice shaking. Her heart just kept racing and the more it sped up, the redder her face became and the dizzier she felt.

The net curtain, jammed in the window, was obvious this time when Erin went back into her bedroom. Her head swirled as she staggered across the room and nervously opened the window. The three individual tracks running down the lower roof where Brodie had lost his footing and slipped were also plainly obvious. She had to get out to the garden.

Just at that time, Mr Stewart stepped out into his garden and called for Rusty.

Erin gasped in horror. 'Rusty! Of course.' Mr Stewart had let him out before dinner. A lost haggis and a mad dog on the loose - what hope did Brodie have? Erin heard a noise behind her and wheeled around on her mother like a rabbit who was caught in the dazzle of a car's headlights.

'S-s-seems like Rusty's gone missing. I heard Mr Stewart calling and looked out to see what was wrong.'

Brenda nodded silently at her daughter, but Erin's nervousness told her that she was worried about something more than just Rusty missing, especially as she didn't like the dog. She simply smiled at Erin and continued along the hall to the bathroom. She'd have to be patient and tease it out of her over the next few days.

A twisted knot formed in Erin's stomach at the thought of a scraggy mutt having a real haggis platter when everyone tomorrow night would be eating the age-old traditional synthetic recipe.

The front doorbell rang powerfully.

Goosebumps broke out on Erin's trembling skin as she sprinted down the stairs to answer it, nearly tripping on her own feet as she went.

'Ooooh Erin,' said Mrs Stewart with the back of her hand at her forehead like she was going to faint. She was wrapped up in a long, camel coat that didn't quite match the green gardening boots she had on her feet. 'We seem to have lost darling Rusty - and on a cold night like this too - my poor, poor baby. Mr Stewart is still searching our garden, but Rusty's paw prints show that he must've snuck through the gap in your hedge.'

There is no gap in the hedge, thought Erin as she turned to announce Rose's arrival. 'Mum … it's …,' but Rose pushed past Erin into the hall before she could finish her sentence. William appeared from around the corner, scowled at Erin and pushed past her as he brazenly followed his mother into the Scott's kitchen.

A puzzled expression formed on Ralph's face as he entered the kitchen too. 'Rose?'

'Hello again Ralph. We think that Rusty has come into your garden through the gap in the hedge. He doesn't seem to be in our garden. Can I take a look?' she demanded. Ralph scratched his forehead, slightly annoyed at Rose's attitude, and led the way to the backdoor. Rose followed him closely and continued to moan about her poor, poor Rusty being out in the cold, cold night.

Erin closed her eyes slowly as Rose trudged across the lawn towards the hedge. Ralph's face filled with horror - he never let anybody walk on his lawn in such cold, wet weather. But, who could stop Rose - or who would dare try? His face dropped at the sight of the gaping hole in his prize hedge. Erin threw her father a knowing look and then scanned the garden for any signs of Brodie.

'There - he did come through to your garden - those are his paw prints!' Rose shrieked. The fresh fall of snow had almost covered them, but she was right. They were Rusty's prints.

Brenda smoothed her hand across Ralph's back to console him as they watched Rose trudge around the garden. They shrugged their shoulders and eventually joined her in the hunt for Rusty as they followed the dog's faint prints up to the holly bush.

'That's as far as they go. They don't go back from it or around it. They simply stop there,' said Ralph curiously. His eyebrows knitted together. 'Aye, aye. What have we here?' He bent down and picked up Rusty's black, emerald-studded collar and a fresh piece of white heather that was lying inside it. 'Strange. Very strange indeed,' he mused. 'We don't have lucky white heather in our garden.'

'And nor do we,' said Rose abruptly, snatching the collar from Ralph. Annoyance flashed across her face. 'What's lucky about this heather?' she whined.

'Lucky for us, that's what,' Ralph muttered dismissively. Brenda heard him and shot a disapproving look his way.

Rose studied the paw prints. 'He's got to be around here somewhere. His prints don't go back into our garden. What about in the holly bush?'

They all crouched down together and peered into the holly bush. 'Nothing but a vile smell in here,' said Ralph pegging his nose with his fingers.

'Same smell that was down at the loch this morning,' said Brenda holding her nose.

Erin flushed with fear. In just three short seconds, her body went from hot to cold and hot again. Where was Brodie?

'Something's been chewing at the holly - look, there are large gaps in it,' said Brenda crossly as she examined her garden's most prized possession.

'Well, blow me down with a bagpipe, that is the strangest piece of animal pooh I've ever seen,' said Ralph with an air of mystery in his voice. Erin, Brenda and Rose leant over Ralph's shoulder and they all gazed down, studying the pooh from different angles. Erin pulled back and retched.

'Very strange indeed. Rose - is Rusty having some sort of

digestive problems?'

Rose threw her head up primly and glared at Ralph for even suggesting it. 'Not at all! Rusty is immaculate. He'd never do anything like that!'

'Erin - fetch me a bag … and some gloves. I think I'll take it to the vet in the morning for analysis. And, grab the digital camera too - those footprints aren't like anything I've seen either,' said Ralph as he walked around to the other side of the holly bush. 'Two sets of prints - or maybe three, it is hard to tell - lead away from the holly bush, go down to the back garden and out of the gate. Out of the gate?' Ralph was mystified.

'Rose! Rose!'

'Yes Owen? Coming dear!' Rose hollered and walked back over to the hedge. Ralph fumed silently as she trampled all over the garden in her large garden boots, never caring to step on the stones.

'Rose dear. One of our gnomes has gone. It's like … it's like … no, I can't even bring myself to say it.'

'Say what, for goodness sake. Come on - spit it out. Rusty's missing and there are the most dreadful animal … droppings I've ever seen here. And weird prints in the snow. You couldn't possibly have any worse news for me!'

'Rose dear. It's like one of your gnomes has just got up and walked away. You know, the real ugly one. I mean … there are tiny footprints leading from where it used to be. How on earth … I can't … oh, I've had too much whisky!'

Rose wailed. 'My poor, poor Rusty. It has to be somebody playing a prank.'

'There's got to be a rational explanation,' said Ralph rolling the heather's stem between his finger and thumb and pensively rubbing his newly shaven chin with his other hand. 'I mean, just where did this heather come from? If we'd only found a collar, well then we could say Rusty had slipped it.' And I wouldn't blame him, he thought examining the piece of gaudy, trinket-studded leather.

Ralph looked up at Brenda and winked mischievously before clearing his throat. 'Rose ... I'd hate to have to tell you this, but, it's probably looking like kidnap.' Brenda threw him a menacing glare and signalled that he was supposed to be helping Rose, not hindering her.

'Kidnap? Owen! Owen! You need to investigate a kidnapping!' With a look of utmost horror, she snatched the collar back from Ralph and ran into the house, through the kitchen, along the hallway and out of the front door wailing at the top of her voice, leaving the Scotts standing in the garden in stunned silence.

'I must tell Owen now! The kidnappers might want money - oh my poor, poor Rusty,' Rose wailed into the night. William, who had been standing silently at the back door through all of this, looked rather embarrassed as he followed on after his mother.

Brenda fought back a smile, looked at her husband who had an expression of innocence painted on his face, and then burst into buckets of laughter. 'KIDNAPPED?! What *were* you thinking of Ralph?'

'Look, darling,' said Ralph through a half serious glare although he found it difficult not to smile. He straightened his back, composed himself and spoke with concern. 'It's very serious.' But he couldn't contain himself either and nearly burst his sides laughing. 'It's about time that darn dog disappeared!'

Laughter rang around the garden for some time and once Ralph had wiped his face dry with the sleeve of his jumper, his voice took on a more concerned tone. 'Seriously, though,' he said through slight coughs as he cleared the laughter from his lungs. 'Don't you think it's all a bit strange?' He coughed once again and thumped his clenched fist against his chest.

Erin stopped laughing and her thoughts returned to Brodie as she looked silently around the garden, trying to understand what had happened. Brenda was still giggling and returned to the kitchen to make supper. Ralph took a few more photos of the prints in the snow and followed Brenda inside, leaving the bag of mystery droppings, tied tightly, in the utility room close to the back door. He set the camera on the breakfast bar. Erin followed, reluctantly, and watched the triangle of light shining on the snow narrow to a slit as she closed the back door. The garden was in darkness.

Erin's stomach knotted tightly as she wondered what had become of Brodie. 'Is there a hole under the holly bush where Rusty went? Maybe a rabbit hole? You know there are always rabbits in the garden and you can't find where they're coming from,' said Erin rising slowly from the kitchen table after she'd finished the mug of hot chocolate her mother had made for supper. 'Not that I have any interest in Rusty,' she said quickly, 'he's an awful mutt and his disappearance is a relief to the neighbourhood.'

'Erin!' said her mother, startled at her outspoken comment.

'Sorry Mum - but it's true and you know it is,' said Erin shrugging her shoulders and glancing at her father for moral support.

'Yes - she's got a point there,' said Ralph curling his mouth and eyes into a smile that made his nose look smaller. 'And if there's any justice, Rose Stewart will be the next to disappear.'

'Ralph! Don't encourage our child - you should know better.'

Ralph slapped his own wrist like a scorned child and as he turned away from his wife, he winked at Erin and put a finger quietly to his pursed lips. Erin returned a hidden smile before kissing her parents good night and retiring to her room - it had been a long and intense day and it hadn't ended yet.

Normally an electric blanket and warm duvet was Erin's favourite time of night in the winter, but she couldn't think about enjoying that or sleeping. The bedroom door clicked open ten minutes after she had climbed into her bed. She shut her eyes and pretended to be asleep. Brenda's shadow formed across her bed as the light from the hall trickled into the room. After the door clicked shut, Erin flicked her eyes open and lay awake listening to her mother moving around the top floor of the house. It was an hour before the house eventually became quiet. Erin looked at the clock. It was midnight. She waited for another half an hour to make sure her parents were asleep, then threw back her duvet and jumped out of bed fully clothed. No amount of tiredness would hold her back from searching for Brodie.

CHAPTER THIRTEEN

The Ghillie Dhu

Erin stared back at the darkened house from the bottom of the garden. It was peaceful. A faint trail of grey smoke escaped from the chimney and the smell of burning peat gave her a warm, homely feeling. Her parents hadn't heard her sneak out and she'd left a note on her bed for her mother to find in the morning saying that she had gone to the loch for a walk. That wasn't unusual for Erin.

The recent snowfall had almost covered up the mysterious prints that meandered from the holly bush to the bottom of the garden; they were just barely visible. Erin had erased all the photos of the prints from her camera and had buried the bag of animal pooh at the bottom of the rubbish bin. A chilling winter breeze chaffed her face and swept her mop of red curls backwards, leaving tiny deposits of ice on each strand. After pulling on her woollen hat and fastening her blue Berghaus jacket and hood tightly around her, she climbed over the garden gate, to avoid the hinges squeaking when she opened it, and headed away from the house.

The moon acted like a nightlight as it shone from behind some white puffy clouds and reflected brightly on the white countryside so she didn't really need to use her torch. The two sets of footprints, one Brodie's, stopped not far beyond the garden wall. Erin bent down and brushed away some snow with her gloved hands.

'I knew it - a rabbit hole.'

She looked up from the hole in the ground and fixed her eyes on the dark forest in front of her. A large, black cloud formed above the trees. She looked harder. It wasn't a cloud. It was a flock of ravens. Brodie must be in there - but who did the other footprints belong to? Without another thought, Erin ran as fast as she could through field after field until she was at the edge of the forest.

The icy air cut her raw throat like a knife as she gasped for breath, and her legs felt wobbly after the hard sprint through the snow. Just like earlier on that morning, a whooshing sound ran through the rowan trees - the sound of leaves being rustled by the wind. But again, there was neither wind nor leaves. Erin stared long and hard into the treetops.

'Why do you come at this late hour human girl? You could be in danger.'

Erin was relieved to see the petite dryad. 'Did you see Brodie come through here?'

The dryad looked saddened as she lowered her eyes and bowed her head. 'No, we did not.'

'I need to find him. I'm frightened in case he's in danger.'

A tear formed in the dryad's eye. 'He is in danger. We couldn't stop him - he entered the forest underground.'

'Underground? In the rabbit burrow?'

'I wish I could say yes - but it's Gnogard's burrow. You know - the gnome. He's been living for years in the garden next to yours as a dumb and reasonably happy gnome. He normally goes out at night to look for some goods to steal, but he's been happy until now.'

'What? Why? Oh, I don't understand you,' said Erin desperately.

'Let's say, the witch,' the dryad spoke hesitantly as she looked into the forest. 'Let's say the witch has done a deal with Gnogard to bring Brodie to her.'

The now familiar rustle of leaves echoed around the treetops. The dryad sounded panicked. 'I've become too involved already, I have to go. Be careful, young girl. Be careful who you trust and don't believe everything you see.' The nymph-like form merged back into the tree and the rustling stopped immediately. All Erin could hear now was the snow falling through the trees. It was too quiet.

'Don't believe everything you see? Geezo, I haven't believed anything I've seen since I met Brodie at the loch yesterday,' Erin muttered as she crept warily into the dark forest, shining a short pathway in front with her torch as the forest grew darker.

It wasn't too long before Erin saw some light ahead. She stopped and peered through the trees towards the glade. There was laughter - haggis laughter - and other laughter from strange-sounding voices. Erin shut off her torch and crept stealthily towards the glade; a glade she'd strangely never noticed before.

Brodie looked to be safe and happy. He was sitting with a number of strange-looking characters, but everything seemed to be friendly. The glade was brightly lit by some means, but not by light bulbs. It was almost like daylight, except Erin couldn't see the sky above - just thousands of light forms. It had stopped snowing, but oddly, there was no sign of snow in the glade itself.

Erin's breath curled in front of her as she studied the group of weird-looking characters. She instantly recognised Gnogard with his extremely wide grin and sheep-like teeth, and eyes so wide apart that they were almost on the sides of his head. His nose was a small dot in the middle of his face, more like a large wart. His head rolled back in raspy laughter, sounding like someone who'd smoked all of his life. But he hadn't - it was just his gnomish sound. He grinned widely at Brodie.

'So Brodie - where on earth do you haggises hide away these days? Haven't seen one around here for centuries. My ancestors were great friends of your ancestors - it's really nice to meet you at long last.'

Erin tensed at the question.

Brodie shuffled about, but didn't answer.

'Sorry there pal, didn't realise it was a secret,' Gnogard said in an apologetic, but joking manner as he paced up and down in front of him.

'Y-yes, well it is a secret, but,' Brodie said pausing. 'I suppose it's ok to tell you. You did save my life tonight from that dog thing back there.'

Gnogard's jaw twitched and an evil smile played around his large mouth. The forest became deathly silent as the group of weirdo creatures waited for Brodie to spill the beans.

'Well …' said Brodie hesitantly.

Erin felt a strong surge of panic and rushed forward to stop Brodie from talking. 'Brodie, no! Brodie - don't say anything! They're not your friends. They're working for the witch!' The torch fell from her grasp and shattered as it hit a tree stump.

Brodie tumbled backwards off the log he had been sitting on and landed in a tangled mess on his head. Erin rushed to his side and helped to untangle his legs from his oval body and brushed the peat from his face.

'Thank goodness you're safe.'

Brodie was confused. 'Yes, of course I'm safe. Why are you so worried? Anyway, thank goodness you've arrived. We've been waiting for you for ages. Gnogard over there said that he had a safe place to take me until you arrived. He was right. Of course he's my friend - he saved my life!'

The forest spun in front of Erin's frightened eyes as she realised she'd walked into a trap. A trap set by the ugly gnome that had lived next door to her for many years.

'Good evening Erin, why don't you join us?' Gnogard smiled widely and revealed all of his large, stained teeth. His brown eyes crossed as he glared challengingly at her.

'That's enough Gnogard. You can go back home now.'

Everyone swung around towards the squawky voice. A small, pixie-like man dressed in a mass of leaves stood in front of them, emitting an air of stern authority. 'I can take it from here - you've done your job - well, almost. And the information about the heather is a bonus - I'm sure I can ask Gertruda to make you even less ugly than what she was going to. Go on - beat it.'

Hurt suddenly flashed through Gnogard's large eyes as he seemed put out by the tone of the ghillie dhu's voice. He clenched his dirt-engrained hand into a fist, wanting to punch the malice out of the green-faced pixie's eyes and he hesitated, looking long and hard at Brodie and Erin.

'Nice knowing you Brodie - you're a hoot - or you hoot, whatever. I'm not sure what I've really done here and can only apologise for my greed and obsession to look handsome. You gotta understand - I've been like this for a hundred years and I know there's new spells that will make me more handsome for the next two hundred years of my life.' His sincerity was quickly replaced by an evil chuckle before he dived back into the hole in the ground from where he and Brodie had entered the forest almost two hours ago.

The evil-looking, evil-sounding ghillie dhu turned to the dozen or so giggling heather pixies whose delicate transparent wings flapped continuously as their heather-coloured eyes sparkled mischievously.

'And you lot - go back to your heather-clad moorlands - you've served your purpose tonight. I'll call on you again when you're needed. You know the punishment if you're in here without me inviting you in.' His words were harsh, but they seemed to rush past the heather-pixies who continued with their pranksterish giggling and obediently filed out of the forest, one by one.

The last pixie in the file looked back at Brodie and hesitated, a tinge of sadness showing in his eyes. The ghillie dhu glared at the pixie and he immediately swung back to the others and zipped through the forest after them.

'Suppose it's my time to go too,' said the urisk who had, until now, remained hidden as he emerged from the shadows of the forest. Brodie's stomach curled at the extreme ugliness of the skinny creature and Erin covered her eyes with her gloved hands to stop her from looking at him. His wrinkled skin was covered in patches of brown hair and hedgehog pins protruded from the folds of wrinkled skin on the back of his neck. His bulbous eyes blinked slowly in his large, misshapen head. There was almost something goat-like about his head and legs, as if an old man was trying to emerge from a goat's body.

'What do YOU think?' said the ghillie dhu coldly, his bogie-green eyes narrowing to fine slits. 'You've had company - what more do you want? Get out of my forest and go back to haunting your pond. I'll call on you when you're needed again.'

The urisk stood timidly as he blinked widely at Brodie and smiled from the wrinkled gap in his hideous face. Brodie tried to smile back, but he felt nauseous. He was frighteningly ugly - there was no doubt about that. The urisk took a few steps, then hesitated before turning back to Brodie.

'Young haggis - I predict that you are in grave danger. Be careful. Call me if you need my help.' He shot a glare at the ghillie dhu. The ghillie dhu reached his moss-covered arms out and they kept stretching and stretching until they were almost around the urisk. The urisk turned and bolted into the forest, knowing that once he was within those arms, he'd be enslaved by the faerie for ever and never be able to roam free again. The ghillie dhu, who was a guardian tree spirit, particularly disliked human beings and hated anyone, or anything that disturbed his precious forest. He turned slowly towards Brodie and a cruel smirk twisted his pixie-like face. He had a long-term score to settle with the haggis.

After the urisk had left, Erin took her hands from her face and exchanged horrified glances with Brodie before fixing her eyes on the ghillie dhu. 'What do you want from us?' she questioned nervously.

The ghillie dhu's merciless laugh echoed around the frosty night air of the forest, then his bogie-green eyes became luminous as he stared at Erin. 'I'm fed up to my back teeth of you trampling through my forest and singing as you do. And my teeth go a long way back, so I do have some patience.' The ghillie dhu pushed his neck out and opened his jaw widely to show his teeth, which went beyond his mouth and disappeared down the back of his throat. He seemed proud of the fact and eventually closed his mouth and wiped the dribbling saliva from his chin.

'You can't sing and you keep destroying my precious ground with those horrible feet of yours. But, I'll deal with you later. It's this beastie I'm more interested in here,' he said coldly, turning his hardened stare to Brodie.

Brodie shivered and through naïve innocence, asked the moss and fir covered pixie a question, which maybe wasn't such a good idea.

'Why, what have I done wrong?'

The green fir leaves quivered as the ghillie dhu shook with great frustration. 'It's not what *you've* done - it's what your ancestors did to my great grandfather!' His eyes widened and cast a green glow over Brodie. 'They sent him mad! Mad, mad, MAD! Instead of being able to protect his forest, he was reduced to a bumbling, nervous wreck anytime anyone or anything entered the forest. He'd jump around and hoot and blubber and giggle and slaver like a lunatic. His behaviour became so bad he was banished from the forest.' The trembling ghillie dhu paused briefly and darted his eyes around the glade. His pointed nostrils flared and his voice hardened.

'A ghillie dhu being banished from his own forest is unheard of so I owe it to his dignity to settle a long-term score with the haggis.'

Brodie shivered at the sound of the ghillie dhu's merciless tone. Erin edged closer to Brodie, also shivering.

'The day those McHaggertys discovered haggis meat ...'

Brodie screeched and his fur and ears stood up straight.

'What's wrong - don't like the thought that you're meat?' The ghillie dhu gritted his teeth in a callous and twisted smile as he continued. 'The day those McHaggertys discovered the haggis, they set to the hillside to hunt you out. But you outwitted them and took cover in this forest and dug burrows under these beautiful trees. My great grandfather not only had to put up with the cries from the trees as you burrowed through their roots, he had to put up with your outrageous snoring. He couldn't sleep!' The ghillie dhu looked traumatised.

Erin suddenly couldn't help but raise a smile at the ghillie dhu. She and Brodie were possibly in serious danger, but the small pixie-like creature laying down the law to them and complaining about snoring was just too much for her. It was verging on comical. All she needed to do was get up and walk away. She had to be dreaming.

'And then,' the ghillie dhu continued to wail, 'when the McHaggertys realised that you were in the forest, they began hacking it to pieces bringing the trees intolerable pain and my great grandfather intolerable noise and heartache! I feel nervous and sick just thinking about it.' The ghillie dhu's voice increased to a high-pitched shriek and he found himself reduced to a bumbling wreck, sobbing uncontrollably. 'It was all too much for him - he tried to enslave the haggises, but he was too weak by that stage.'

The bright lights that were shining from above the forest suddenly dimmed and a cold breeze blew against Brodie's face. The ghillie dhu stopped crying and his eyes grew dark and serious.

'But you haggises also annoyed someone else - someone far more powerful who would never forgive what you did to her.'

Brodie hunched his shoulders as he strained to listen to the ghillie dhu's fading voice against the increased wind around the glade. Erin leaned down and cupped her hand around Brodie's ear as she spoke to him.

'Come on, we don't have to listen to this. Let's get out of here.' There was worry in her voice and Brodie instinctively followed her. They took two cautious steps backwards before turning and running towards the east of the forest. Everything went dark as though someone had turned off the lights.

'Going somewhere?' A green glow surrounded the ghillie dhu as he stood in their path, smiling dangerously. Erin and Brodie turned and started running towards the west side of the forest.

'I don't think so,' said the ghillie dhu waggling his long, green finger at them. He was in their path again, still glowing an eerie luminous green as his arms stretched towards Erin. 'Once I have you in my arms Erin - you'll be enslaved to me forever. Someone else wants Brodie even more than I do.'

Erin screamed as the ghillie dhu's arms extended around her. 'Run Brodie, run!'

Brodie was about to jump up and sink his teeth into the long arms when a spine-chilling cackle pierced the silent air in the glade behind them. The ghillie dhu looked disappointed. His arms shrunk back to their normal size and hung limply by his sides.

'It's ok Booger, I'll take it from here.'

'Aw, will you stop calling me Booger!'

'Well, you look just like something that's been sneezed out - Booger suits you. Move over - my turn to have some fun.' The mysterious voice cackled insanely as a dim light returned to the glade.

Brodie and Erin swung around and were startled to see a small, stone cottage across the far side of the glade. Had it been there before and they just hadn't noticed it? Green-tinged smoke rose in puffs from the crumbling chimney. A black, cloaked figure stood in front of the open doorway, silhouetted by the orange glow that lit up the windows on each side of it. The mysterious voice spoke in a cruel and heartless tone.

'We meet again … Brodie.'

CHAPTER FOURTEEN

Gertruda McNorris

Brodie's pulse increased rapidly as a sudden feeling of déjà vu flowed through him. The blood drained from his face and his energy waned as two flame-red pupils burned into him. He wanted to close his eyes, but they were paralysed.

Erin noticed what was happening and quickly ran between Brodie and the silhouetted figure. 'Don't stare at its eyes. They're sucking the life out of you.' The burning stopped immediately and Brodie squeezed his eyes shut to relieve the pain.

Dozens of large ravens swooped down onto the slated roof of the battered-looking cottage; others lined the treetops and some remained patrolling the sky, squawking threateningly. Erin ducked slightly as one swooped across her and stole the woollen hat from her head, dropping it at the feet of the mysterious cloaked figure before perching brazenly on its crumpled shoulder.

'Smart girl we have here Booger.'

'Too smart for her own good. I want her as mine - you have to allow me that much, Gertruda.'

'Welcome back,' the voice crackled from beneath the hooded cloak. 'It's been a long time … Brodie. Please - come closer.'

Erin and Brodie exchanged nervous glances and stepped backwards instead of moving towards the cloaked figure.

'You heard the lady - move closer.' The ghillie dhu rounded up behind them, forcing them closer to the cottage.

'Closer still, I need to see you better - my eyes aren't so good these days.' The woman's evil cackle sent shivers down Brodie's spine but seemed to instil energy into the ravens as they flapped their wings vigorously, almost as if they were applauding her.

As they reluctantly moved closer, Brodie and Erin could see more than just a silhouetted figure. It was a woman. Her breathing was shallow and rattled disgustingly in the back of her throat. A spindly, wart-encrusted hand emerged from the folds of the dirt-engrained cloak.

Erin shrieked and Brodie ducked in behind her legs to hide from the gruesome figure. They gawked, mouths wide open, as the hood fell from the woman's head to reveal a very dead-looking witch … who was very much alive. Black hairs growing from the large, lumpy wart on the end of the witch's hooked nose seemed to be wiggling on their own like small fingers. Another lumpy wart hanging off the end of the witch's pointed chin wobbled from side to side as she spoke. Her thin mouth slowly widened into what can only be described as a smile to reveal two blackened teeth.

'Yes, a bit of an ugly cow, aren't I?' she cackled. 'It's not nice feeling this way. As soon as all the haggises in the world are dead, I can finally rest in peace. If I'd known how long it would take, I'd never have put the wretched curse on myself,' she muttered regretfully before snapping her dark, empty eyes back to Brodie.

Brodie swallowed sharply. The strangest feelings flushed through him as the witch's merciless eyes bore down on him.

'I wasn't always like this, you know. And it's because of you stupid, ugly little haggises that I am. I cannot die until I know you're all mincemeat!' Erin blinked sharply and jerked her head back as the witch spat the words at them. Gertruda's heavily lined, ghostly face slackened into a calm smile and she tilted her head to one side as she examined Erin more closely.

'Do you want me to do it now, Gertruda?' asked the ghillie dhu in a servant-type tone.

'Oh, just behave yourself you stupid moss-ridden pixie. You know the plan, just shut up and bide your time. I'll tell you when you're needed … Booger.' Gertruda waved her hand dismissively and returned her gaze to Erin to soak in her prettiness.

'I was almost as pretty as you, Erin Scott, and very likeable too at that. Until,' she snapped turning her reddened gaze to Brodie. 'Until those haggises ruined it for me!' The ground below them trembled as Gertruda stomped her foot and formed her skeletal hand into a tight fist. The enormous, crusted wart on the end of her chin throbbed bulbously against her dead-looking skin. Then she reverted to calm again and paused, smiling briefly.

'I, Gertruda McNorris, was engaged to be married to Alexander McHaggerty, the son of Henry and Elizabeth McHaggerty who lived in the big house at the edge of the forest. It's not there now,' she said, an evil grin contorting her face. 'Ah bless, not a McHaggerty left. They all perished in the fire. Alexander did love me dearly though,' she crooned memorably.

'I wasn't as pretty as most, but Alexander McHaggerty saw my inner beauty - I was a very kind, very caring woman. But,' said Gertruda darkly, 'I was the daughter of an old woman who lived in this cottage behind me, where I have now lived for hundreds of years!'

'Old woman?' Erin asked warily as Brodie listened on. She took a small step backwards and Brodie moved with her.

'Aye, lass. She was an old hunchbacked woman, like me, who was banished to the forest away from the locals. Such a tragedy for a woman.'

'What tragedy?' asked Brodie peering out from behind Erin's legs.

'Oh … being ugly like this,' said Gertruda in a bittersweet tone with an almost pitying expression on her face. 'Mind you, you'll know all about being ugly, young Brodie,' she cackled.

Brodie stuck his neck forward and growled at the witch. Erin kicked him sharply with her boot and he ducked back in behind her legs.

Gertruda continued to smile menacingly at Brodie as he peered out from behind Erin's jeans. 'I am the last in a long line of witches to have been banished to this place. I didn't have any children - I turned like this before I got the chance to even be married,' she said sadly and drifted off into her own world bumbling over words that Brodie couldn't make out.

Erin took another step backwards and Brodie moved with her.

Gertruda lifted her eyes and her face hardened as she spoke through a steely voice. 'We try to live as normal people and only use our magic in our own circles. We're generally good witches, until something angers us greatly. Then, we turn into the meanest of black witches and are only happy from other people's misery.' Gertruda cackled loudly and stroked the wart on her chin with her bony fingers as the memories flowed through her mind.

'I remember it as clear as day. My mother was dressed like a princess for the autumn festival ball that was up at the grand McHaggerty house.' Gertruda looked at Erin and sighed wistfully. 'She looked beautiful and most people at the ball thought so too - stunning.'

Brodie watched Gertruda's craggy face change throughout her tale. One minute it was as hard as nails, the next it had taken on a sweet, almost baby-like expression.

'My mother was leaning against the balcony just above the wonderful banquet of food as she chatted to my father. Then the stupid railing gave way.' Gertruda wept. 'My mother fell, face first, into the food. Cream was clotted in her shiny, black hair; red jelly was smeared all over her beautiful dress and mustard was wedged up her nose. Do you know, not one person ran to help her? They all just turned, pointed their ghastly fingers at her and laughed.' Gertruda blinked away a tear as she pointed her finger into mid air and stared at it silently before snapping it back into her fist.

'Until then, nobody knew that she was the daughter of the old witch in the forest. She wasn't able to control her anger. The transformation into a black witch took place in front of their eyes and everybody stared on, horrified and sickened by what they saw, not least my father. He turned us both out to the forest and told us never to return, but before we left, my mother infested every one at the ball with head lice.' Gertruda laughed spitefully. 'The only way they could get rid of it was to shave their heads, tee hee. They were told worse would happen if they ever disturbed us.

'And there we lived for years with nobody bothering us so the last anyone saw of me was when I was a pretty six-year old.' Gertruda snorted and sighed memorably. 'But my mother would sometimes create havoc in the village with her spells. I tried to keep her as good as she could be, but there are sometimes when you just can't control your mother.'

Erin took another step backwards. Brodie moved with her and then looked at Gertruda sharply. 'So, what happened to you?'

The witch's discomfort was obvious as she breathed in deeply through her nose and cast Brodie a deathly look before responding.

'The only way we can be rid of this curse is to have three generations of witches controlling their tempers. After the third generation has succeeded in not transforming into … this form … then the curse is lifted and we become white witches forever. Sweet, isn't it?' Gertruda's nose curled and her eyes hardened.

'But I never managed it! My sister has, her daughter has and now her granddaughter must keep control of her temper and then the curse is lifted on her children after she has died. But, I'm not so sure she's managing too well - she's signed up to these new-fangled anger management classes. As if! What's the world turning to?' Gertruda rolled her eyes, horrified at the thought.

Erin took another step back from the witch. Brodie shuffled back with her and continued to talk to Gertruda.

'But how come you never made it …?'

Red flashed through Gertruda's eyes and green slime dribbled from the corners of her mouth as she wept. 'You're an inquisitive, impatient and thoughtless haggis. It's very disturbing for me … but not half as disturbing as things will get for you.'

CHAPTER FIFTEEN

Trapped

Erin and Brodie gasped at the sight of the witch's snarling face as she waved her withered arms above her head insanely. The fir trees in front of them began to sway violently and two large creatures with small, fat wings emerged from them and circled the sky above the glade. Each creature had the body of a lion, the beak of an albatross and growled like a Rottweiler.

'Get them!' shouted Gertruda as she pointed to Brodie and Erin.

Brodie yelped as the large claws of one of the creatures dug into his back. Erin screamed as the other creature sunk its claws into her shoulders and soared into the air.

'Meet Dork and Klutz they're absolutely gorgeous, aren't they?' Gertruda broke into uncontrollable laughter.

Brodie looked down at the ground below him as he dangled from Dork's claws.

Erin thrashed around trying to free herself from the strong grips of Klutz's claws, but she tired very quickly. She looked to Brodie as he continued to stare at the ground, feeling giddy from the height.

Gertruda continued to cackle loudly. 'Now, if I may continue? I can't stand the ignorance of anyone trying to leave before I've finished my story. Dork. Klutz. Set them back down on the ground - closer to me this time. I don't think they're going anywhere - are you?' Her twisted smile stabbed at Brodie's insides.

The two bird-like creatures dropped Erin and Brodie to the ground like stones. Brodie rolled back onto his feet and quickly faced the witch. Erin raised herself from her knees to full height and moved close to Brodie. They gawped at Gertruda. She was one dead-looking witch.

'Aahhh - where was I before I was rudely interrupted?' Brodie could almost see the last few frames of the story run through Gertruda's eyes like a filmstrip as she reminded herself of where she had got to.

'Yes, handsome Alexander McHaggerty - very handsome in fact - was thrown from his horse just outside the forest one day and I was there to help him and nurse him back to health. Of course, he fell instantly in love with me and my lovingness to a complete stranger. I didn't tell him who I was or where I lived. I lied and told him that my father would not let me have a boyfriend, so we agreed to meet secretly at the same place. He rode to the edge of the forest daily to visit me and the fact that he didn't know anything about me made him more interested in me.' Gertruda sighed miserably.

'One day he invited me to a huge banquet in my honour so that I could meet his parents. And at that very banquet, he announced that he was going marry me. I was as surprised as everyone else, but over the moon.'

'So you just agreed to marry him?' asked Erin in disgust. 'Without even discussing it?'

Gertruda looked shocked. 'Dear, dear - to be asked to marry someone is a great honour - do not forget that.'

Erin rolled her eyes at the thought of falling at the feet of any guy just because he asked her to marry him. 'And then I suppose you lived happily ever after?' she asked sarcastically.

Erin's words were like knives through Gertruda's heart. 'How dare you make a fool of me. If we'd lived happily ever after,' she spat stepping towards Erin and Brodie, 'do you think I'd be here today looking like this and feeling like a piece of dried up old boot leather, never being able to leave the forest? Huh?' Saliva spat from her crinkled mouth as she continued to rant.

Brodie's heart quivered as the witch moved closer to them,

her eyes now an endless black and the corners of her mouth twisted back into her face. Grey folds of skin on her jaw flapped loosely as she continued.

'I was able to keep my identity from him for almost a year. A whole blissful year. And then you appeared!' She pointed a trembling finger at Brodie.

Brodie swallowed sharply and shrieked like a girl as globules of sweat broke out over his body and trickled down his back.

'Yes, you furry heather rat! That's what you are, you know - a heather rat! After the McHaggertys discovered one of you, they wanted more and took to the hillside to hunt you down. You apparently taste very nice … but when you came into the forest to hide, they followed you and … and Alexander found me in this cottage with my witch of a mother!' Gertruda lowered her face into her hands and sobbed.

'He was outraged that I had deceived him - that he was engaged to be married to the spawn of a witch. He cast me aside. I begged him not to. Begged him so hard. But he cast me aside with so much hate.' Gertruda's grave sobs echoed around the trees and then her head flopped back as she suddenly cackled loudly.

'Oh what fun, what fun! The moment he did that, I naturally lost my temper and turned into what I am now - right in front of his eyes and I cursed his family for ever.' Gertruda's voice softened to a child-like whisper and she cupped her hands together gently nursing nothing more than fresh air. 'Until that day, I'd never harmed so much as a spider.'

'But,' said Brodie hesitantly as he looked into Gertruda's dark eyes. 'What's that got to do with me now?'

Gertruda flew into a rage. 'I had no daughters to carry on my vengeance. So I vowed to live on until every haggis was dead. DEAD, DEAD, DEAD!'

Every piece of fur flattened against Brodie's body as he cowered from the witch.

'If it wasn't for that … that interfering white witch, Noremac, well … I'd have killed all haggises and died peacefully a very long time ago. But Noremac paid the price for interfering.'

Noremac? Erin mouthed to Brodie, arching her eyebrows as she remembered him saying her name back at the house.

'But, as I failed to do what I set out to, I vowed I'd never give up my hunt for the haggis until I'd killed every last one of them,' said Gertruda screwing up her vile face and leering at Brodie. A large, glistening blob of saliva trickled down her chin and dangled from the pulsating wart before splashing to the ground. Then a softer tone entered her voice once again and a friendly smile played around her mouth as she looked at Brodie. She drummed her fingers against one another.

'And that's why you want to kill the haggis? Because of Alexander McHaggerty? Because you lied and got found out? You're despicable!' said Erin hotly.

Gertruda rounded on Erin and pointed at her strongly. 'Shut your mouth you imbecile. I'll deal with you later - or, Booger will,' she cackled. The ghillie dhu laughed with her as they leered at Erin.

Gertruda fixed her eyes back on Brodie. 'So, Brodie. You're going to be a nice wee haggis and tell me where I can find the rest of your kind.' Her evil cackle grated on Brodie's nerves as she edged closer to him. 'Then, I can rest in peace. PEACE I tell you! What a wonderful thought after all this time. You know, I felt your presence the moment you reappeared and my energy … and my friends,' she said smiling up at the ravens, '… drew you to me.'

The ghillie dhu jumped up and down clapping his hands excitedly. His menacing laugh sent chills through Brodie's bones as he remembered the force that had dragged him through the loch at high speed until he was spat out of the water onto the shore. He remembered the terror that had whooshed past him as the incredible force kept pulling him further and further away from Nessie. Of course, it had been Gertruda's energy.

'Quick Brodie,' hissed Erin. 'Gertruda can't get out of the forest unless she's invited. Follow me - run fast and don't look back.' Brodie looked from Erin and then to Gertruda. He nodded at Erin and they turned and ran to the left of the glade.

A bright, red light flashed in their path and forced them back.

'What now?' shouted Brodie.

'Just keep following me!' Erin ran further along the glade before making a dash for the trees, but again they were forced back by a flash of red light that instantly melted a hole in the snow just beyond the glade. The ground was left smouldering.

'Not so fast, Erin sweetie. You've no way out of here - alive.'

Breathing hard against the frosty night as they searched frantically for a way out, Erin and Brodie turned around just as two beams of red light left Gertruda's eyes and bounced off the forest floor inches from their feet. The witch threw her head back and cackled insanely.

'There is no way out - you're trapped! Ha, ha, ha, ha ....'

CHAPTER SIXTEEN

The Silent Protector

Ravens began swooping down on Erin and Brodie, forcing them back to the centre of the snowless glade. The ground just inside the glade began to erupt and hundreds of small, peaty-brown boglouts, no more than a foot high, dug their way to the surface. The small, devilish creatures lived below the ground in peat bogs around the forests and thrived on disruption and mayhem. Their brown, beady eyes shone sinisterly as they arrived in an array of giggling gabber and an army of them quickly formed a wall around the glade and dared Brodie and Erin to break through it. Their brown fangs and black claws glinted daringly as their spiked tails thumped the ground repeatedly.

Brodie and Erin rounded on a noise from behind them. A fierce-looking, black panther emerged from the cottage door purring deeply as it walked stealthily towards them, its silky tail swishing wildly. Its head drooped low between its hunched shoulders as it hissed loudly and displayed a mouthful of razor-sharp teeth.

'We're trapped!' cried Erin as a low, menacing growl played around in the back of the cat's throat. 'Where is your Silent Protector when you need it most?'

Brodie looked at Erin helplessly and groaned. He had no idea what it was or if it would ever save him.

'Why Kittikens - dooooo come and join in the fun,' Gertruda cackled, beckoning the large cat with her ghostly white finger. The panther growled and flicked its tail strongly as it padded past Erin and Brodie. They edged backwards and bumped into something. Erin trembled and glanced over her shoulder.

'Boo!'

They both screamed and ran away from the ghillie dhu as he

laughed heartlessly. But whichever way they ran, the ghillie dhu seemed to appear from nowhere and send them back. Ravens swooped down on them, groups of boglouts giggled ceaselessly and bared their brown teeth and claws at them, and Dork and Klutz sat by the cottage looking entertained by everything.

'Come, come children. You've no choice but to give me what I've waited so long for.' Gertruda raised her twisted arm from her cloak and snapped her bony fingers together. Two shabbily dressed, round-eyed goblins emerged from the cottage carrying a small pot between them, green mist swirling eerily from it.

'Well, here's one I prepared earlier. I had reckoned on you not telling me the truth, so I've made up this lovely potion to suck you dry of the truth instead,' hissed Gertruda. Flicking her black cloak, the witch positioned her arm above the pot and lowered her fingers into the green mist. Her eyes shot wide open and turned bright green. Her cloak flicked again and her other bony arm shot into the air and then slowly lowered until she was pointing directly at Brodie.

Erin moved to pull Brodie back.

An electric-green beam of light ran through Gertruda, left the tip of her warped fingernail and connected with Brodie as she mumbled something that Erin couldn't understand.

Brodie shook violently as a strong field of energy surrounded his body. The green light traced an outline around him and a powerful explosion followed as the light connected with the main beam that was coming from Gertruda's hand. A spark of green light left Brodie and hit Erin hard in the head, catapulting her into the air like a cork from a bottle. The seconds felt like minutes to Brodie as he watched her fly through the air and slump to the ground more than ten feet from him.

Gertruda threw her head back and screamed at the top of her voice. 'NOR-E-MAC! Even dead, you're still able to mess up my spells you interfering white witch. I'll just have to kill the haggises one by one as they return to the Highlands. I'll start with Brodie!' She pointed at the sky and then to Brodie. 'Kill him now!'

Hundreds of black ravens descended from the sky and the trees and headed towards Brodie like an arrow from a bow.

Anger rushed through Brodie's veins as he looked at Erin lying to the side of him, motionless. A strong energy dragged him from the present into a whirlpool of mist. This time he saw Noremac's face through the mist, her white eyes full of comfort as she spoke to him in a fragile whisper. Her voice seemed to come from every direction, urging him on.

'I'm here, dear Brodie. Fear not. You'll live on if you feel the power. Believe in yourself.' Brodie wanted to reach out to her, to touch her hand and to ask her questions. But she drifted back as he moved through the mist towards her. She became more transparent as a dark mist began moving towards her. 'Brodie - stay focused.' She sounded weak.

A screeching sound like nails being dragged down a blackboard filled his head, followed by repulsive cackling. Gertruda. Gertruda was in his mind - or his dream - or was it even real? He couldn't be sure. *Stay focused. She said stay focused.* The energy drained from his body as fast as the black mist was trying to smother him. His mind could think of nothing else but to get Noremac back, until he lost consciousness.

The next Brodie could make out was soft thudding on the forest floor and things falling on him. He opened his eyes and uncurled himself. Everywhere around him were clumps of white heather, some still falling like giant snowflakes. Erin had almost disappeared under them. He bounded across the glade and brushed the pieces of heather from her lifeless body and noticed that a black feather was weaved through each piece of heather.

'Well, well - so, it's a declaration of war then is it?'

Brodie looked up sharply at Gertruda. Her grey skin was pulsating with more crusty warts.

'What do you mean?'

'I mean, you've only just reduced my poor, poor ravens to … white heather! You murderer!' Gertruda tilted her head from side to side and stared thoughtfully at Brodie for some time before muttering something to herself and laughing. The goblins that were holding the pot of green mist threw it to the ground and fled the forest with the boglouts following closely behind them. Dork and Klutz looked stupidly at each other, laughed freely and then soared into the sky as they realised it could be them next.

Brodie frowned and scratched at his head as he tried to understand what had just happened.

The ghillie dhu turned and began tiptoeing out of the glade.

'Booger! Don't even think about it. Get yourself over here now,' Gertruda demanded. The moss covered ghillie dhu trembled as he scuttled over to Gertruda and hid behind her.

'Get out from there you coward. We have to fight this pile of haggis fur together. Now - we won't be turned into heather and taken as trophies for anyone, let alone a beastly haggis. I will be nobody's lucky white heather - do you hear. NOBODY'S!' She instructed Kittikens back into the cottage and he seemed to go quite willingly.

Brodie only had vague recollections of what had happened as he slowly realised that he had somehow turned those threatening his life into white heather. Just like the dog. It wasn't Gnogard at all. He had saved himself - so he knew what the Silent Protector was - but why couldn't he remember that he'd used that power and how he'd used it? He looked down at Erin's pale face. Dark rings had formed underneath her eyes and her mouth was tinged with blue. He pushed at her shoulder with his nose. There was no response. He placed his toe-like fingers over her face and eyes, then shook her shoulder again. She was motionless. Brodie felt his heart tear apart. He turned to Gertruda feeling anger that he'd never felt before.

'I mean it, you ginger freak of nature. You'll never take me as a trophy!' Gertruda raised her arm and pointed a long, bony finger at him. The tip of her thick, twisted nail glowed red.

Brodie stared challengingly at the witch, anger set hard in his face.

Gertruda cackled heartlessly and a beam of red light left her fingertip.

Brodie concentrated his eyes on the light. It stopped short of her fingernail, reversed and jolted Gertruda and the ghillie dhu into the air before they disappeared. Two pieces of white heather dropped to the ground. Brodie looked on completely surprised and in disbelief at what had just taken place and he cautiously edged his way over to the spot where Gertruda and the ghillie dhu had been standing. Moss was weaved through one piece of heather. He looked to the other. It seemed to be covered in warts. He smiled cockily as he realised that he had just managed to zap Gertruda. Booger was a bonus. And he'd remembered and seen it all happen.

'Who said I would never take you as a trophy? Seems like I've proved you wrong - witch!' he quipped and picked up the two pieces of heather between his teeth.

The first hint of morning entered the wintry sky. Brodie looked at the cottage and hesitantly stepped into the doorway. A large portrait, almost the height of the ceiling, was hanging just inside displaying a handsome man with dark, penetrating eyes and the words "Alexander McHaggerty" were engraved into a brass plate on the bottom of the wooden frame. She must have rescued it before she burned the house down. Candles flickered eerily in alcoves on either side of the portrait, which seemed to bring Alexander's eyes to life. Brodie shuddered and snapped his head away from the portrait.

As Brodie stepped back from the stone cottage, it began to fade until it had disappeared completely. The peaty, snowless ground under his feet seemed to shrink and pull the fir trees in from the sides until they had closed up the glade. In just a few short moments, there was no evidence of Gertruda ever having been there. Apart from the white heather.

The forest was suddenly drenched in eerie darkness. Brodie turned and dashed back to Erin who lay motionless on the forest floor. Tears prickled at his eyes. He'd never cried before, but he just couldn't contain the deep sadness that he felt inside. His bagpipe wails wound their way through the forest. The best friend he'd ever had was dead and it was all his fault.

'Brodie?'

Brodie stopped crying and looked up through tear stained eyes. His stomach churned at the ghostly sight of the urisk but as he noticed the compassion in his eyes and the broad, vacant smile playing around his mouth he began to see past his ugliness. Brodie looked back to Erin. 'She's dead.'

The urisk knelt down beside Erin's body and placed a dirty hand over her mouth. After a few seconds, he spoke. 'No, not dead. Barely the breath of a butterfly left - I know someone who may be able to help her. But we have to be quick.' He scooped up Erin in his thin arms and struggled to carry her through the forest for she was larger than he. The urisk grunted and puffed and panted until he arrived at the edge of the forest - in the rowan trees - where he gently set Erin down on the ground. He slipped the rucksack from her back.

Brodie had never felt so helpless - he could only follow on and hope that Erin could be saved.

After making Erin comfortable, the urisk stood up and scanned the silhouette of the bare treetops against the dawning sky.

'Dryads … please, we need your help.'

Brodie scanned the trees with the urisk, but nothing appeared.

The urisk pleaded again. 'Dryads - please help us. It's Erin …'

'Brodie. I warned you about the danger that lay ahead. You didn't take my advice.' The dryad raised an arm from the tree and then her head. The familiar rustling of leaves could be heard as the other dryads emerged from the surrounding trees, their faces filled with grief as they stared at Erin.

'Please, dryad - help this young human girl. She is a good person, but nearly dead.' The urisk dropped to his wrinkled knees and grabbed Erin's lifeless hand. His skin was very wrinkled from spending too much time in his pond. 'Please - I know you've helped others.'

'But not humans.' The dryad looked to Brodie. 'You were warned.'

'Please - don't blame Brodie. He's innocent in all of this. He needs help, not lectures. Can you help Erin?'

The dryad looked at the urisk for some moments as she nodded slowly and thoughtfully before continuing, now with urgency in her voice. 'Ok. But you have to be quick. Place her right hand on the tree and then stand well back. This is a risk for both the girl and me.'

The urisk did as he was instructed, but Erin's hand flopped to her side. He tried again, but it just flopped down to the ground.

'Hurry up!'

Desperation filled the urisk's eyes as he looked up at the dryad. 'Can't I just hold it to the tree?'

'No!' said the dryad impatiently. 'Quick, time is running out. If you touch her with even your breath when I'm transferring energy, you'll suck both of us dry of energy.

Brodie paced around in desperate circles and his insides squirmed in tight knots as he prayed for her safety. 'I've got it! Tie her hand to the tree with that green thing that's around her neck,' he said urgently.

'The scarf?'

'Yes, quickly. She mustn't die. Hurry!' Brodie pleaded.

The urisk snatched the scarf from Erin's neck, slapped her hand against the tree and wrapped the scarf around it and the tree. It worked.

'Now quickly - stand well back.' The dryad turned to another two dryads in the trees beside her. 'I may need your help if I don't have enough energy for Erin.'

They nodded obediently.

The dryad's brown eyes rolled back in her head as she concentrated on transferring her energy through the tree and into Erin.

Erin's hand jumped as the energy entered her body. The dryad shook slightly. Erin shook slightly and her skin changed to resemble the bark on the tree. Then it flickered back to her own and then back to bark.

Brodie whimpered as his limp friend fought for her life, never taking his anxious eyes from her for even a second.

The dryad threw her arms out to the side. 'I need more energy! I'm losing her!'

The two other dryads reached across from their trees and grasped her hands tightly. A strong wind blew through the branches and lightening flashed overhead. All three trees budded; spring leaves formed, thousands of red berries grew and turned quickly to dried, brown berries that dropped off with the autumn leaves until the trees were bare once again. The wind stopped blowing and the three dryads broke their circle and flopped against their trees, exhausted.

'We can do no more Brodie. We need rest. Urisk - be sure to bring us some of your pond water.' The dryads' eyes were drained of energy as they slumped back against their trees. Brodie and the urisk looked into Erin's motionless face and waited for a response. It seemed like an eternity. But there was nothing. Not even a twitch.

'I'm very sorry young haggis.' The dryad spoke sincerely through a weak voice as she feared the worst.

Large tears welled again in Brodie's eyes and he hung his head in sorrow. The urisk placed a hand on Brodie to console him, but nothing could. His heart had been broken beyond repair. He may have freed the haggis from Gertruda's curse, but he'd helped take the life of an innocent girl in the process.

Deeply saddened, the urisk untied the scarf and gently placed Erin's hand over her chest. A pale spark flowed between them and Erin's body jolted. Warmth seeped slowly back into her body. Brodie stared on silently as he saw colour return to her skin.

'What happened?' Erin croaked softly as she lifted her head and strained to focus her eyes.

A relief that Brodie never thought he would experience washed through him as he saw the life return to Erin's eyes. 'You're alive!'

'Or course I am Brodie - what happened? How did I manage to fall asleep?' She shuddered and jerked her head back when she saw the urisk standing over her, but the warmth in his eyes told her that she didn't need to worry.

'Erin - you need rest,' whispered the dryad. 'You need to reserve your energy.'

Erin stared up at the dryad above her. She looked drained, somewhat older.

'Don't worry, we'll recover. But I must warn you there is still much danger ahead of Brodie. Never underestimate Gertruda.

Don't believe everything you see, but make sure you believe everything you feel. Now go - all of you. We need our rest too.' The dryad's eyes closed and she merged back into the tree. The familiar rustling of leaves echoed around the forest and the other dryads faded into their trees. The forest was silent once again.

'But … Gertruda's dead,' said Brodie in a confused whisper.

Erin stared on in bewilderment. 'Dead?'

Erin and the urisk listened to Brodie as he related the story of his battle with Gertruda and he finished by proudly displaying the pieces of heather to them. When she regained the feeling in her legs, Erin stood up and patted the trunk of the rowan tree.

'I can't ever repay you for what you've done for me.' The dryads didn't appear. There wasn't even a rustle. But Erin didn't expect anything the dryads were exhausted She turned to the urisk and bent down and hugged him. His grotesque features became transparent through the most appreciative smile she had ever witnessed.

'And I can't ever thank you enough or repay you for what you have done for me. I'll never forget you.'

'I've enjoyed your company, human girl. And yours,' he said turning to Brodie. 'If you ever need me - you know where to find me.' He sighed heavily and sadness touched his distorted, wrinkled face. 'I am happy to serve you again.' He appreciated friendly company and reluctantly waved them off from the forest.

As Erin waved back to the urisk she noticed that her watch had stopped again - just like before. Her eyebrows knitted together in a frown. 'Strange.'

'What?' asked Brodie.

Erin considered telling Brodie, but she decided not to. He'd never understand anyway. Shrugging her shoulders dismissively, she began the walk back home. Her arms and legs were like lead weights as she trudged through the snow. She was exhausted.

So was Brodie. He came close to losing the best friend he'd ever had. It was time to go home.

CHAPTER SEVENTEEN

A Misty Night

Erin turned the heather over and over in her hand as she stared thoughtfully out of the kitchen window. She was only now coming to terms with how close she had come to death and was finding it all very difficult to believe. After carefully examining the heather that had been found the night before in their garden, Erin noticed that small pieces of Rusty's fur were weaved throughout it which she hadn't noticed before. It was all that was left of the dog. She gently replaced it on the windowsill and moved her hand to the note her mother had left.

> *"I left you both to have a long lie it's going to be a long day. Will be back around three. The taxi will pick us up at seven o'clock tonight. Will phone you later. Love you both, Mum xx"*

As Erin replaced the beige notepaper on the windowsill she looked at her watch. It was working again. She checked the time with the clock on the cooker. It was the same. How could that be? Her eyes closed briefly as she shook her head, trying to make sense of everything that had happened. It was all too confusing.

Grabbing some fruit and biscuits from the cupboard, Erin wearily climbed the stairs to her room. Her father was gently snoring as she passed by his bedroom. After pulling back the duvet, she lifted Brodie out of the rucksack and set him in her bed. He didn't waken. Her bare feet sunk into the thick carpet as she padded across the room to the window and scanned the countryside with her tired eyes. A heavy sky descended over the day. Everything looked normal. Peaceful. Apart from the shuddering memories of the past few hours. Grabbing the folds of the heavy green curtains with both hands, Erin heaved them together snapping out the light instantly. She threw on her pyjamas after discarding her clothes untidily on the floor and slid under the duvet beside Brodie. After three seconds, her eyelids closed and she drifted into a much-needed sleep.

*

Brodie woke out of his comfortable unconsciousness to the sounds of thumping. As he put his mind in order he realised it was the sound of knocking on a door. But he wasn't entirely sure where he was.

The door clicked open.

Ralph saw a burst of Erin's red hair poking out from the top of the duvet and smiled warmly. 'Erin?'

Brodie tensed under the duvet as he recognised the voice.

'Erin? You ok?' Ralph walked over to Erin's bed and pulled the duvet back from her head. 'It's mid-day, love - I've never known you to sleep so long. Are you ok?'

Erin's eyes flickered opened and she moved them around trying to focus on her father. Her mind was blank and she felt at peace, although very tired. She yawned widely.

'I've never heard you snore before either especially as loud as that. Maybe you're coming down with something. Are your sinuses blocked?' Ralph pressed the skin around her nose with his thumb and index finger.

Everything suddenly rushed back to Erin like a steam train running through her body and her stomach cramped violently when she remembered that Brodie was under the duvet with her. Erin snatched the duvet from her father and pulled it up tightly around her neck.

'Yes Dad,' she said quickly. 'Maybe you're right. I'll get

up soon and have a hot shower to try and steam it out of me. I don't want to be ill on Mum's special night.'

'And yours too - Daniel Radcliffe, eh?' Ralph teased playfully.

Erin had another panic attack. That's right. Daniel Radcliffe was going to be there tonight. She'd have to start getting ready now!

Brodie was ignorant to everything going on around him. He just had a burning desire to be back at home, away from the bright lights and noise of people. His mouth had become very dry and his stomach gurgled hungrily as the smells of food drifted up from the kitchen but images of centipedes dampened his taste buds.

Erin looked at her father innocently and then patted her stomach through the duvet.

'Sounds like you need some of my broccoli soup for lunch,' Ralph said and then left the bedroom.

'Thanks Brodie. Now Dad thinks I not only snore like a haggis but that I'm as hungry as one.'

'Good morning to you too!'

'We've missed that – it's afternoon. I'm not letting you out of my sight until I manage to get you back to where you came from. You're coming everywhere with me and you'll have to come to the Burns Supper tonight as well.'

Brodie groaned. 'When they're all eating haggis? You can't do that to me. And Gertruda has been dealt with, so I'm out of immediate danger.'

'Look - it's not real haggis. You're coming - no arguments.' Erin laughed to herself as she looked at Brodie's blue eyes, the ginger-red fur that covered his body, his three strange legs and the most unusual nose she'd ever seen. 'I am actually arguing with a haggis. What next? A straight-jacket?'

Chuckling insanely Erin jumped out of bed, sprinted across

the room and hauled open the curtains. The extreme daylight almost knocked her off her feet as it poured heavily into the bedroom. The sun had finally broken through and the snow on the trees and walls was beginning to melt. She moved her gaze across the hedge to the Stewart's garden. Gnogard had returned to his place by the other gnomes, still looking as ugly as he did before. A satisfied grin crossed Erin's sleepy face. Gertruda would no longer be able to give him the good looks he was hoping for. Justice was well served. But her grin soon disappeared when she observed the heavy cloud of mist lying over the loch. Sighing despairingly, she turned to Brodie with a grim expression on her face. 'There's no chance of you going home tonight if that mist doesn't clear.'

*

Ralph had insisted that Erin wear the clan tartan, but she had argued if she had to wear any tartan, it would be a colour she liked. She pulled on a long, pleated skirt and matching bolero-type jacket that had designer pleats down the back. The collar stood up stiffly around her neck and her hair was pulled up in swags at each side of her head and fastened with matching tartan clips. She admired the colour and smiled smugly.

'It's nice that you can change the way you look just by wearing different clothes and doing something with your long fur,' said Brodie, in awe of Erin in her green tartan. 'You look simply … different.'

'I can dress you up in tartan if you want?'

But Brodie backed off shaking his head. Clothes looked like too much hassle.

When the green winking light on the charger flicked off, Erin lifted her camera from it and packed it in the side pocket of her rucksack along with her autograph book. The least she could do was get a signature from Daniel.

Erin's father knocked on the door. 'Taxi's here.'

A sensitive moment followed as Brodie sighed and looked at Erin. He reluctantly climbed into the rucksack and watched the light fade as Erin drew the ties together. She pulled on her coat, hauled the bag over her shoulder and snapped off the bedroom light before descending the stairs, careful not to trip on her skirt.

The car tyres scrunched over the snow in the driveway as the taxi pulled away from the house. A large, yellow snowplough boomed past them shovelling snow into the driveway and blasting the front of the car with grit from its spreader. The taxi driver began to curse, but stopped abruptly when he caught sight of Brenda's stern glare in the rear view mirror. He pulled onto the road and fumed silently. The icy night and the slow moving traffic made the drive to Urquhart Castle longer than usual.

Eddies of mist rose eerily from the dark surface of the loch.

'Ah, the mist,' said Ralph with a deep and distant stare towards the loch, just barely visible. 'You know what they say about the mist …'

Erin rolled her eyes and yawned. 'Yes. It's all to do with the so-called thermocline that lies about a hundred feet down in the loch. Apparently the water above the thermocline can alter the temperature. But it really depends on weather conditions. It hardly ever alters from about forty-five degrees fahrenheit below the thermocline. The nearer the surface water becomes to freezing point, it sinks and is replaced by warmer water from below. That's what creates the mist,' said Erin tartly as she rattled off the facts she'd read on the Internet. 'So there's nothing mysterious about the mist and there's no bogie man about to appear out of it.'

'Smart cookie you have there,' said the taxi driver. 'I'd prefer to leave a bit of mystery to the mist … scotch mist … eerie, cold and … monsters …'

Brenda rattled her red, polished nails on the armrest and threw the taxi driver another annoyed look. 'You may not be scaring my daughter - but I scare MUCH more easily.'

The driver apologised quickly. 'Sorry, Mrs Scott - but you're husband did start it.' Brenda raised her eyebrows at Ralph and shook her head at a loss. They were supposed to be two grown men, not six-year old boys.

Having never been in a car before, Brodie began to experience motion sickness. His stomach bubbled and gurgled as the car swayed gently along the road. He felt close to bringing up his last meal. He'd never felt so sick in his life.

The indicator ticked loudly when the driver eventually pulled the taxi off the road into the car park at Urquhart Castle. The place was buzzing with activity. Large men in dark suits and kilts patrolled the entrance and some photographers were milling around, waiting to snap some high-class photos. Erin shied away from them and circled her arms around her rucksack to protect Brodie.

'Oh Erin, that scruffy thing spoils your lovely outfit. Why didn't you leave it behind?' said Brenda wearily as she eyed the black rucksack which still had slight stains on it from the raven pooh. Her day had been hectic with last minute changes and anxious phone calls from agents and celebrities enquiring about the weather. But Brenda had reassured everyone that the weather wasn't as bad as it sounded and that all roads were open. She went to take the bag from her daughter but Erin grabbed it tightly and threw her mother an exasperated look.

'Mum. It's got my camera in … and a change of clothes because I know that I'm going to feel too stuffy in this. And some things to do in case I get bored … I need it with me.'

'Well, put it behind you for now. We're going to get our photo taken.' She circled her arm around Erin's shoulders and pulled Ralph in beside her.

'Smile,' said the tall man behind the camera.

Brodie jumped as the bright light from the camera flashed through the mesh. It gave him sudden thoughts of Noremac and how she had died protecting the haggis from Gertruda.

Just as they entered the building, Erin glanced up at the icy, night sky. The clouds had begun to clear and were replaced by star-studded pockets of velvety sky. But, if there was any hope in Nessie surfacing, the heavy mist that continued to hang over the water had to clear as well. A dull heaviness filled Erin's chest.

CHAPTER EIGHTEEN

Robert Burns at Urquhart Castle

Brodie watched intently from inside the bag as Erin handed her coat over to some stern-looking people behind a counter before descending a long, sweeping, spiral staircase. Large pictures of Robert Burns hung from the walls and swags of tartan were draped around the pictures and the wall.

Erin looked around in amazement. Everything looked so different. The entrance way that normally opened out into a tourist shop and a cafeteria was now closed off with a decorative screen of draped tartan and dried heather and thistles, which only allowed access to a corridor that displayed historic memorabilia and the entrance to the small cinema.

'Erin - can you go into the kitchen and give this cheque to Mr Gunn for the haggis? His van's outside, so he should be around somewhere.' Brenda pushed a brown envelope into Erin's hand. Her mobile phone burst into life once again and she turned and sashayed along the corridor with it glued to her right ear, waving her left arm descriptively and at the same time checking that everything was as it should be. A gracious smile remained on Brenda's face as she spoke into the phone. 'Yes, yes. Everything's looking splendid so far - we just need the guests to arrive. That's going to be the most nerve-wracking of all ... I'm so excited ...'

Erin eventually found her way into the kitchen where dozens of people in white aprons were tripping over one another and raising their voices, steam was rising from pots (and some people) and someone had just dropped a bowl of cream onto the flagstone floor and was being scolded by the chef.

'Erin!' Harold Gunn waddled his way through the bedlam towards Erin. Brodie's eyes narrowed and he growled low in his throat as he instantly recognised him as the haggis killer. Erin prayed that Harold wasn't going to be reduced to a piece of heather in front of her eyes.

'I caught an army of haggises yesterday. Look, it's all cooking well here,' he said lifting the lid on one of the large, stainless steel pots. Steam bellowed into his large face and he jerked his head back, blinking his eyes to clear the steam from them. Small droplets of water now covered his skin. 'Well, I think I'd have cooked it a bit better than this …'

'Oi!' The chef, a tall, slim man with a white, buttoned tunic and white hat reached across from the other side of the cooker and slapped Harold's large hand with a steel spatula. 'Your job is to shoot the beasts. Mine is to cook them - so you shouldn't even be in here!'

Harold grunted in amusement at the chef. A mischievous grin twisted his face and there almost seemed to be an element of danger in his eyes. He received great pleasure from being in a busy kitchen and winding up the chef. 'Gotta catch a glimpse of the stars somehow. I'm sure you can't deny me that?'

The large meat cleaver glinted against the light as the chef waved it around, muttering something not too polite about the butcher under his breath, before signalling reluctantly that Harold could stay in the kitchen for just a short time. 'If you're not out in ten minutes, then you'll be mincemeat!' The meat cleaver slammed into the wooden chopping board, but Harold merely chuckled.

The chef's anger was instantly replaced by a pleasant smile as he noticed Erin standing behind the butcher. 'Excuse my manners, young lady. I presume you are Brenda's wee lass?' he said smiling politely. Small beads of sweat dotted his flushed-looking face.

'Yes. I'm Erin,' said Erin holding out her petite hand to introduce herself and she returned a shy smile.

The chef wiped his slim hand down his apron before shaking Erin's hand. 'I'm Shugie. Pleased to meet you Erin. I haven't cooked for so many famous people at once, so things are a bit tense in here - apologies. I would like to stay and chat, but I must get on.'

'Sorry - Mum sent me on an errand to give this to Mr Gunn - I can see you're busy. Nice meeting you.' Erin handed the brown envelope to the butcher who gruffed a laugh before jamming it into his shirt pocket and winding his way back through the kitchen and out of the door, his large bottom wobbling from side to side after every step he took.

'Well that's a large relief,' said Shugie as he stared after Mr Gunn. 'That man's been trying to tell me how I should be cooking haggis - I've been doing it for years for goodness sake! Years!' A loud crashing interrupted their conversation. The chef rolled his green eyes and held his hands to his head before turning and shouting orders at a woman who'd dropped a pile of cooking utensils.

Erin quietly slipped out of the kitchen. Brodie had by this point curled up at the bottom of the bag and plugged his ears. Human life was far too disruptive for him.

By the time Erin returned to the corridor, dozens of very well dressed and good-looking people were milling around the curved corridor chatting to one another, sipping either champagne, Glenmorangie or orange juice and nibbling at shortbread as they glanced at the historic memorabilia that was displayed behind the glass wall. The air was buzzing with a cocktail of different accents and everybody was dressed in tartan of varying colours and styles. Some were in traditional Highland dress; others had obviously allowed their designers a free reign to create something different, as long as it was made of tartan. Her gaze suddenly faltered and her heart flipped.

There he was - Daniel Radcliffe - looking very masculine and handsome indeed in his kilt and white jacobite shirt. Erin gasped and stood admiring him as many famous people bustled past her, unnoticed. She stared at the expensive-looking sgian dubh knife that was strapped to his calf and the unusual sporran that hung around the front of his kilt. She frowned and squinted her eyes as she looked closer at the ginger-red sporran. It had a face and a body, and three legs hung from it. Erin shuddered. It was so like a dead REAL haggis it was uncanny. Ant and Dec moved in to talk to Daniel and blocked Erin's view. She only hoped Brodie hadn't seen the sporran - if it frightened her, he'd probably turn Daniel into heather! There was no way she would get anywhere near him for a signature now.

'Are you ready?' said Brenda running her hands over Erin's hair to tidy it up. 'Have you seen young Daniel over there?' She smiled and nudged Erin's arm. 'Like his sporran - very unusual.' Erin flushed with embarrassment.

At that moment, a lone piper entered the corridor and began to play the bagpipes.

Brodie's eyes crossed over and his brain vibrated with the excruciating noise from the piper.

The babbling of voices from the crowd fell to a hush and everyone turned and watched the tartan-clad piper appreciatively as he piped his way around the corridor and up the steps to the cinema. Brenda grabbed Ralph and Erin and followed the piper, and everyone else filed into the room after them.

The plain walls were graced with pictures of Robert Burns and large boards displaying some of his best work. A large, tartan curtain took up the wall at the front of the cinema. The air smelled of a heavy concoction of perfume and aftershave. Erin sat at the back of the room with her parents and surveyed the backs of all the rich and famous heads with interest. The lights dimmed and a white screen lowered from the ceiling. The first of two short films began about Robert Burns and the history of Urquhart Castle.

Brodie had no idea what was happening or any wish to. He was becoming increasingly irritable at all the noise and his body was cramped as he tried to get more comfortable in the bag. Everything had gone dark. He peered through the mesh but couldn't see much. Then he jerked back when his eyes locked onto two sets of round, green eyes. Cowering at the bottom of the bag, Brodie glanced back at the mesh. The eyes stared in at him.

'We want what you've got,' a malicious voice hissed from behind the cold eyes.

'What?' Brodie trembled.

'We want what you've got!' said two voices in whispered unison.

On hearing the gruff whispers, Erin looked down at her feet and gasped at the sight of two green goblins pulling the bag under the seat.

Brodie whimpered.

Erin lifted her foot and stamped on the larger goblin who squealed like a pig. The other goblin sunk his razor sharp teeth into her ankle, then took off with his comrade and ran down the stairs to the front of the room, knocking over a glass of orange juice that was on the floor beside the lady sitting in front of Erin. The lady simply reached down and picked the glass up, never once glancing at the goblins as they rushed passed her and descended the steps in full view before scuttling under the tartan curtain behind the white screen. The curtain moved only slightly - like a small breath of air had ruffled it. Malicious goblin giggles filtered from behind the curtain and Erin looked around in amazement. Not one person had noticed or heard them. All eyes remained fixed on the screen.

The throb in Erin's ankle and the spilled orange juice told her she wasn't imagining the goblins. It would be another ten minutes before the film would finish so she sat with her teeth clenched tightly and her hands curled into fists. Half the battle of getting rid of pain was to be able to scream when it happened, but she hadn't let so much as a whisper pass her lips. Brodie watched the blood trickle down into her shoe. Once again, he was helpless to Erin's needs.

After the films ended, everything became very dark, with only the gargoyle candleholders casting a faint glow around the room. As the large white screen folded into the ceiling, the heavy tartan curtains began to draw apart slowly; a loud gasp filled the room.

'I want that as my back garden. How much to buy this place?'

'Wow - it's magnificent.'

'Incredible.'

The ruins of Urquhart Castle were floodlit against the dark, wintry night and looked more like a magnificent painting on the wall than reality. Its backdrop was the legendary Loch Ness, but it was too dark to see it against all the lights. An energetic rustle followed as everyone dug into their bags and pockets for their cameras.

'Ooh - I see Nessie!'

Laughter immediately rang around the room.

Brodie bolted upright and peered through the mesh as he tried to see Nessie, not realising someone had said it as a joke. Only, he knew she wasn't just a joke. She was real.

Ritchie McTouey, the famous presenter from the local radio station, was the Chieftain for the evening and he stood in front of the crowd wearing not only a dapper of a kilt, but a large welcoming grin on his face.

'After we've had a wee dram and some haggis, we'll maybe take a wee wander around the ruins if the weather holds. We may even be lucky to see the Northern Lights … and Nessie.'

A wave of awe filtered around the room. Brodie felt a surge of panic as he wanted to leave now to look for Nessie.

Ritchie McTouey lowered his hands to hush the crowd before he continued. 'I believe that Rod Stewart was asked to sing Purple Heather tonight, but unfortunately he wasn't able to make it.'

A lot of "aw's" and "aah's" echoed around the room.

'But, we do have a very special treat tonight. Miss Dion Cameron will sing Robert Burns' most famous piece at the end of the night from the castle's tower house - Auld Lang Syne.' A loud applause followed Mr McTouey's speech and a cold shiver ran down everyone's spines as they imagined Dion's famous warbles filtering from the enchanting Highland castle.

'Calm down now Ralph,' said Brenda as she stood in front of him and blocked his drooling gaze.

'Aye, and you can calm down too. I know how you think that Ritchie's Inverness accent is sexy - you can't fool me.'

Erin rolled her eyes and followed her parents out of the cinema as they chuckled like two school children. She'd never understand grown-ups.

The tartan that had been draped on one side of the corridor was now pushed back against the wall and they exited directly into the dining room. The two end walls had been painted to make it look as though they were built of stone. Plaster holders were fixed around the walls to resemble old, stone candleholders and a large, medieval candle chandelier hung from the middle of the room.

Six large oak tables filled the dining room and were flanked by large oak chairs. The tables were set with the finest of antique silver and candlesticks, dried heather and thistle arrangements, tartan napkins bound by solid silver holders of Celtic design, and fans of oatcakes and shortbread ran down the centre of each table.

Erin was astounded at the transformation of the place - she felt like she was in a real castle. The glass wall to the far side of the room led onto the patio where real fire torches were burning strongly against the wintry night. Beyond the patio were the ruins of Urquhart Castle lit up in magnificent splendour - the most romantic Highland backdrop anyone could ever wish for.

'Magnificent castle,' said a tall, good-looking man with black, slicked back hair. He had a soft, American accent and seemed very interested in the castle.

'Yes, it's an absolutely fabulous place. Your first time in Scotland?' said Brenda, shyly. Erin craned her neck to absorb the man's handsome features and realised that her mother's flushed face wasn't due to the champagne. Even she blushed at how handsome he was. He seemed familiar to her - probably from a movie she'd seen. Brenda looked somewhat relieved to be interrupted by the headwaiter.

The "ooh's" and "aah's" continued for the next half hour as everybody checked the seating plan and found out who they were sitting next to. Erin was stuck on a table between her mother and father.

'Why didn't you hand your rucksack to the cloakroom attendant?' said Ralph as he placed a glass of orange juice on the table beside Erin and smoothed his kilt against his legs before sitting down on the high-backed chair. Erin screwed her face up and shook her head, tucking the rucksack under the table at her feet. She left the top open for extra ventilation for Brodie.

All Brodie could see were men's black shoes, cream kilt socks, tartan dresses and the most expensive and challenging range of ladies' shoes ever, all encrusted with gems, some of which were made to look like thistles. He became intrigued in a green pair of shoes that resembled Nessie, with her long tail spiralling up around the lady's ankle and half way up her tanned calf. He marvelled at the likeness.

The constant buzz from the many guests chattering away,

and glasses clinking as they toasted one another grew louder as time moved on. As if that wasn't intolerable enough for Brodie, his head felt like a hammer drill when someone rattled on the table above him with a large spoon.

'Could I have silence please everybody,' said Ritchie McTouey through a loud and commanding voice. Most of the chattering died down and eyes turned towards him. Mr McTouey gazed around the room and cleared his throat. After a few elbow prods from friends, the remainder of the voices quietened down and all eyes focused on him. He nodded appreciatively and a wide grin divided his face. Waiters' tartan kilts swayed silently from side to side as they weaved their way around the tables clearing the empty glasses.

'Thank you for all being here on this 25th day of January to celebrate our best-loved bard - Robert Burns, or Rabbie as we fondly call him. Born in 1759, he died at a very young age in 1796 … a prize for the first person who can work out his age!' Hearty laughter echoed around the room. 'Sorry, just kidding. There is no prize. I'm feeling a tiny bit like I'm back at work on the radio speaking into this microphone. It's a real honour to be asked here tonight and it's an even bigger honour to be able to eat haggis with so many famous,' he said pausing deliberately, 'and rich people. Some of you will know the format of the evening. But for those who are new to it,' he said in his broad Inverness accent, 'well, we'll be toasting all the lovely lassies, and we can't forget the address to the haggis … oops, nearly forgot. And for those vegetarians among us, I'm told that there is a vegetarian equivalent to the haggis made up of all the vegetables a haggis usually eats. A haggis is a vegetarian, you know? I make a point of only eating vegetarians.'

Laughter filled the room once again.

'OK, so we're about to pipe the haggis in … before we rip it apart and eat it.'

Brodie groaned miserably and tried to blank his mind of the haggis platter.

'The little blighters were a wee bit more difficult to catch this year, I'm told - I think they're playing us at our own game now. So, once the piper has stopped, I'd like you all to raise your glasses to address the haggis that we managed to catch.'

Brodie squealed and looked around him. Who did they catch?

A piper, followed by two waiters carrying a large, steaming haggis on a tartan-draped hod, began playing his bagpipes as he led the hod-carriers around the room. Everyone began to clap in time with the pipes, some people whooped and some whistled.

Brodie didn't know how much more churning his stomach could take or how much longer his heart could put up with the constant fear he felt. The bagpipes continued to grate through his bones and he had an overwhelming sense of urgency to get himself out of the room before they started eating the haggis. He couldn't tolerate the noise anymore - it was torturous - like a hundred haggises were dying inside his head. As he scrabbled inside the bag to plug his ears, it toppled over and Brodie rolled out onto the floor. As he crashed into a table leg, he gently brushed against a woman's foot; the one wearing the Nessie shoes. Her foot immediately catapulted out in front of her and kicked Brodie across to the other side of the table.

The woman then looked on in disgust at the man sitting next to her, raised her hand and brought it hard against his face.

'What was that for?!' the man asked perplexed, holding his hand over his stinging cheek.

'You know perfectly well what that was for!' the woman shrieked. 'You pervert, you!'

Brodie fell onto a man's legs this time. The man turned admiringly to the woman sitting next to him and smiled as he set his hand on her knee. The woman shrieked and returned a slap across his face, and thereon Brodie was systematically kicked from side to side under the table as he continued to clamber over feet in his desperate bid for freedom.

The commotion worked its way along the entire table, with most men protesting their innocence, some facing law suits and others finding new friendships. One rather old lady took a shine to the young man next to her and placed her crinkly hand on his knee. She smiled at him admiringly, her eyes virtually disappearing into her many wrinkles. The young man immediately jumped up to avoid her advances and crashed into one of the waiters who was carrying a large, silver tray laden with full glasses. The tray and expensive glasses crashed to the floor and sent reverberations around the room and through Brodie's head.

Brenda's whole insides sunk to below her knees and she lowered her head in her hands as she saw months of organising come crashing down around her ears. Ralph simply smiled and looked on in amusement. He thought it was the most entertaining night he'd ever seen.

Erin suddenly realised what must have happened and slid down her chair and under the table.

'Brodie!'

Brodie turned back to Erin as he just managed to avoid another kick. She waved him back. He contemplated the moving assault course before tripling his way back to Erin, narrowly avoiding a barrage of legs and feet. Erin bundled him back into the rucksack and slipped out of the room unnoticed. The last thing she witnessed was her mother having words with her father when the lady next to him accused him of feeling her leg.

'Well - that will probably go down as one of the most memorable Burns Suppers ever - and all caused by a haggis!'

Brodie's ears were still ringing from the noise and his stomach churned nauseously. He was exhausted. He just wanted to go home - to be with his family. His drooped ears and eyes jerked upwards when goblin laughter suddenly echoed around the corridor. Brodie and Erin darted their eyes anxiously as they quickly scanned every crevice and corner they could see. There was nothing, except goblin laughter.

CHAPTER NINETEEN

The Witch Hunt

Brodie sprung from the rucksack and leapt to the floor. 'Home. I must get home.' His voice quivered as he ran away from Erin and began scaling the stone steps of the spiral staircase. Robert Burns seemed to glower down at him as he passed portrait after portrait that hung from the walls.

Erin panicked and ran after him. 'Brodie - come back. It's not that way.'

But Brodie never heard. He continued to scale the stairs trying to wipe everything from his mind that had happened to him over the past two days. He stopped short of the top and gasped breathlessly.

Two pairs of green goblin eyes stared down at him, evil smirks spread across their faces. Brodie shrieked and bumped into Erin when he rapidly descended the stairs.

'Goblins!' he said jumping around furiously. 'G-g-goblins!' He began to wail uncontrollably as he darted around in a tizz. His eyes grew wide when he looked over Erin's shoulder. 'MORE! They're down there too!' he yelled nodding down the stairs.

Erin now saw the goblins descending the stairs towards them. She looked behind her. Two more goblins were making their way towards them, their ugly faces creasing as they burst into sinful laughter. Brodie looked back up the stairs. The goblins were closing in on them.

'Quick Brodie - do something with your magic!' said Erin sharply.

Brodie hesitated.

'What are you waiting for? You've got the power.'

Brodie swallowed heavily and shook his head. 'Easy for

you to say. I'm not even sure how to use it!' He wailed again.

'We want what you've got,' said one of the goblins descending the stairs.

'Give us what we want and we'll leave you alone,' said another goblin climbing the stairs behind them.

Erin and Brodie looked up the stairs, then down the stairs, then exchanged horrified looks. Erin shifted awkwardly and her eyes grew troubled as she deliberated what to do. A layer of hardness formed on her face and she turned purposely to the goblins below.

'Stop, you green bunch of slime balls!' she instructed. There, she'd said it. Spoken to goblins for the first time in her life. They stopped and blinked widely at her, exchanged defiant glances with each other and then burst into rapid, garish laughter as they slapped one another on the back.

Erin stamped her foot in anger. 'Will you please stop laughing at me!'

The goblins turned and stared pointedly at her, their green eyes burning into her skull.

Erin folded her arms across her chest and dropped her hip on one side. 'I want to know how come no-one else saw you back there in the cinema?'

The eldest of the goblins cleared his gravelly throat and stepped forward. 'It is only those who believe that will see us.'

'Believe in what?'

'Believe in the faerie world of course - like you do.'

'But I don't,' Erin protested placing her hands on her hips.

A dangerous smile crept into the goblin's lumpy face and his forehead crinkled down over his eyes in a deep frown. 'Oh but you doooo. And once you're a believer, you can't go back. Now give us Gertruda!' His eyes glowed determinedly.

'Give them what they want - and maybe I'll have a chance

of looking handsome one day.'

Erin and Brodie swept their eyes upwards. Gnogard descended the stairs and joined the goblins, a boyish grin playing around his grotesque mouth.

'Maybe then I'll be able to find someone and fall in love.'

'Maybe if you were a nicer person … er … gnome … then you'd have fallen in love a long time ago,' said Erin nastily.

A low, growling sound formed in Gnogard's throat as he gritted his stained teeth. 'Just do as you're told, human girl and we'll leave you alone - gladly!' He spat a piece of soil onto the floor.

A wave of panic surged through Brodie as he saw terror enter Erin's face. He'd landed her in enough trouble and now she was in even more. 'Erin. Please? Give it to them,' he pleaded.

Erin's face remained hardened as she dug into the rucksack for the two pieces of heather. 'What do you want with a piece of useless heather?'

'As long as we have her with us, we can try and get her back some day.' Gnogard signalled to Erin to hand the heather to the goblin.

A shiver grumbled through Brodie's stomach and a strong rage suddenly rushed through him. He snarled like a wild boar and bared his teeth. 'You will NEVER get Gertruda back!' He looked like a haggis with rabies.

The goblins looked slightly uneasy and babbled away in some goblin language. Turning back to Brodie, they raised their hands and clicked their fingers and dozens of peat-covered, sniggering boglouts immediately joined them from what seemed to be out of nowhere.

Brodie stopped snarling and watched the faeries close in on him and Erin as they were about to be crushed.

'Do something Brodie!' said Erin with urgency in her voice,

flicking her eyes from left to right as she gauged the time they had left before they would be mauled by faeries.

'Like what? I don't know what I'm supposed to do!' Brodie felt helpless.

'Just give us what we want and we'll leave you alone.' Gnogard returned a short and nasty laugh and stepped closer to Brodie.

Erin chewed on her lip as she wondered what to do. She could either shut her eyes and pretend that none of this was happening, or give them what they wanted. Her ankle was still throbbing from the goblin bite earlier on. No, they were definitely real. She couldn't pretend they weren't there so she reluctantly reached into the rucksack and pulled out the two pieces of heather. 'Suppose you want Booger too?'

A raucous laugh erupted. 'Him? We've been trying to get rid of him for years so that we can live peacefully in the forest. You've done us, and Gertruda, a favour there. Keep the little snot bucket - with our pleasure.' The goblin grinned cruelly and stretched his upturned green hand in front of Erin. The boglouts copied him.

Brodie stared at the upturned hands. He wasn't giving up his trophy without a fight. The moment they had Gertruda back, they'd be sure to get an antidote to the spell and the haggis would be in danger once again. He had to do something. His head spun and everything became a blur.

The heather quivered in Erin's hand as she stretched out her arm nervously and closed her eyes. The goblin moved forward and lifted the white heather from her palm with his nail-bitten fingers. The faeries cheered triumphantly.

Erin jerked her eyes open. The last things she saw were the goblin's triumphant eyes smiling at her before he disappeared. Two pieces of heather - Gertruda and the ghillie dhu - floated to the floor and joined the dozens of other pieces of white heather that lay scattered across the stairs, some speckled with green and some entwined with peat. Erin's heart tripped when she saw Brodie's motionless body lying on the stair. She bent down and placed her hand on his shoulder, shaking him gently.

'Brodie?' Relief spread across her face when he stirred.

'What happened?' asked Brodie, blinking his eyes in a dazed confusion.

'You mean you don't remember?'

'Remember what?'

Erin spent the next few moments talking Brodie through what had happened. 'You know, it seems that this spell makes you forget any enemies you've encountered. No wonder you've never believed you had any enemies. It's plainly obvious.'

The immense tiredness Brodie felt seeped from his body as he stretched his limbs. 'Seems like I need to be very angry as well as frightened to work the magic,' he said kicking at the heather with disgust. Then he remembered the kelpie and how he had been slipping in and out of consciousness before the vortex had allowed him to escape. Had he been about to use his powers then?

A door banged from below.

Brodie jumped as he returned his mind to the present.

Erin sifted through the pieces of heather, retrieved the one she wanted and quickly tucked it into her bag.

'Is everything ok?'

Brodie was on full display. He froze almost to stone. Erin scooped him up and clutched him tightly in her arms as she rounded on the woman. 'Huh?

'Is everything ok? Ooh, what's that you have there?' The tall, elegant woman spoke in a soft and endearing voice. There was much tenderness in her eyes.

Brodie became trance-like and remained motionless, barely

breathing or blinking as he watched the white blur in front of him.

Erin fumbled for words. What could she say? How was she going to explain this one? She'd never believe he was the latest in dogs. 'Errr … he's a haggis. Uhm … I collect unusual stuffed toys. You can buy them from the local gift shops,' Erin blurted out.

'A haggis, eh? Wow. I must look for one before I go back. He's really cute, in a funny sort of way.' The woman's soft, pink lips curled into a half moon smile as she swept her eyes around the floor. 'Wow - all this heather. It's lucky, isn't it?'

Lucky for me, Erin thought and smiled uneasily. She was a bit awestruck at the beautiful woman standing in front of her, dressed in a white ball gown that was draped with an unusual tartan of white, pink and green.

'You must be Erin? You look just as your mother described, with such beautiful, red hair - very Scottish. Can I have this?' she asked picking up a piece of the heather - the only one entwined with moss. It will go with my dress and will bring me some luck when I have to sing later on. I've just seen the Northern Lights - they're beautiful. Hope they're still twinkling when I'm singing.'

Erin nodded silently, too nervous to utter any words.

'You take care and I'll see you at the castle later. I must go and warm up these vocal cords before your mother decides to fire me even before I start.'

Erin nodded and watched the woman glide back down the stairs. As if anyone would dream of sacking Dion Cameron, she thought rolling her eyes back in her head.

The woman swept along the corridor singing her way through the musical scale and was gone in a swish of white and pink tartan as she rounded the corner.

'Noremac,' cooed Brodie.

'What? No, that was Dion Cameron.'

'Noremac.'

Erin grabbed Brodie and shook him by the shoulders. 'Snap out of it you daft haggis. What on earth are you on about?'

Brodie's eyes were glassy. He smiled stupidly, like he was drunk. 'Noremac - she just visited - didn't you see her? A bright light. I couldn't see her fully, but she was swaying - just in front of me. She warned me of danger.'

'Brodie - I only saw Dion Cameron standing in front of me. What are you on about?' Then it hit Erin like a lead brick. 'Noremac! But of course! Why, it's the reverse of Cameron … and Dion … it's … it's Gaelic for *protection*. No way … it can't be.'

'Say what?' said Brodie confused once again by human babble.

Erin stared down the corridor briefly and looked back to Brodie. She scratched at her nose, squinted her eyes and shook her head dismissively. It had to be a simple coincidence, that's all. Brodie was just dreaming. Dion Cameron couldn't be Noremac. But Erin felt she could believe just about anything right now.

'Come on - we need to get down to the shore - jump back in,' she said holding the rucksack open for Brodie. 'You got off with it once, but if someone else sees you, they'll be addressing ***you*** in the dining room.'

It took Erin just under a minute to gather up the pieces of peat-threaded and green spotted heather. She willingly deposited them in the bin before sneaking into the kitchen.

Plates of haggis and clapshot were being whipped away from the kitchen at high speed by the tartan-clad waiters and the chef was customarily waving his arms above his head as he shouted at his staff. Erin ducked behind the steel workbenches and crawled along the flagstone floor on her knees, her long kilt holding her back a little. The kitchen's back door was now in sight so she stood up to a crouch and made a dash for it, but her heel caught in the hem of her kilt and she stumbled, grabbing on to a rack of pots that came crashing to the floor.

Brodie thought he'd been shot between the ears.

Erin grimaced and her body flushed with embarrassment as a deafening silence fell around the kitchen and the blethering that had been filtering through from the dining room immediately stopped. Two large, black shoes appeared at her nose as she lay motionless on the floor, barely breathing. She looked up at the assistant with pleading eyes and pressed her finger to her lips. The young man glared down at Erin with narrowed eyes and then looked back to the harassed chef.

'Well?' the chef demanded impatiently.

Everyone remained silent, frightened to blink should it make a noise.

The young man looked back at Erin as she lay on the floor, trembling, and threw her a wink. 'Seems like we've a ghost in here. I'll clean this lot up.'

The chef stared chillingly at his assistant. 'I suppose the ghost just came on up from the castle to upset my kitchen then?'

'No, it's probably the ghost of Robert Burns trying to get a quicker service from this kitchen. Will you keep it down in here and hurry up for goodness sake,' said the headwaiter hurriedly as he pointed his finger at the chef.

'The cheek of it! Get out of my kitchen - NOW.'

The steam that had been rising from the waiter's ears reduced to a small puff of smoke. Snapping his finger back into his hand, he turned on his heel, his green tartan cape pirouetting with him as he stomped back out of the kitchen muttering something under his breath about the chef's inability to cook for celebrities - no, his inability to cook full stop.

Nobody dared to even think about raising a smile as the chef nodded to his team to continue, and everything went back to the usual busy mayhem like nothing had happened. Erin returned the young man's gesture with a relieved smile and continued to crawl towards the exit. He walked with her and opened the door whilst he pretended to put a bag of rubbish out. She didn't know why he was helping her, but could only assume it was because her presence in the kitchen earlier had taken the heat off him when he had let a jug full of cream slip through his fingers and crash onto the floor.

The cold, night air hit Erin in the face like a block of ice and she quickly regretted not taking her coat with her as she buttoned her tartan bolero up to the neck. The frost snapped at the skin around her eyes and ears as she made her way down to the loch. Brodie shivered uncontrollably. He was already getting too used to the humans' warm homes.

A shadow moved over at the castle and the orange glow from a match lit up someone's face, momentarily. The outline of Harold Gunn's large frame filled the archway into the castle as he lurked around for a glimpse of some of the A-list celebrities. He was supposed to have left the area before they arrived. There was something about him that made Erin shudder.

It was only minutes before Erin's ears and fingers were numbed by the frosty, night air. She looked around her to make sure she was alone before setting the rucksack down. Brodie jumped out as she rummaged around to retrieve her hat, scarf and gloves before quickly pulling them over her head and hands. As she wrapped the scarf around her neck, a small voice broke the night air.

'You there - stop!'

They both bolted around and rested their eyes on a small soldier who was standing behind them, a few inches short of three feet tall, his right hand raised at them. It was distinctively red.

Erin rolled her eyes in her head and tutted impatiently. 'Not another bossy faerie. What is it that you want?'

The soldier's face hardened. 'I am Ly Erg - an omen of

death. Challenge me and you'll die within a fortnight. Work with me and you will have a second chance.'

'So, answer the lady LY-ERG,' said Brodie cockily. 'What do you want?' He tripled up and down in front of Erin like a guard dog, only with three legs. He wasn't afraid of him, more's the pity, otherwise he could've zapped him into heather.

Ly Erg's red hand lowered and pointed at the rucksack. 'Gertruda.'

'Jings Mc-Crackerty. Another of Gertruda's follies. Well, how's this for a no-brainer. She's mine for the keeping,' Brodie said sternly.

'Be warned, haggis features. Cross me and you'll be dead in less than a fortnight. You have one last chance.'

'We have to get rid of this idiot,' Erin whispered hurriedly.

'Well, I'm not frightened of him or angry with him, so I don't really know how to.'

'We've got to do something. We need to move and quick.'

Brodie flicked at his nose as he thought of Saunders McRancid. No … he couldn't … or could he? He wouldn't normally excuse that sort of behaviour, but there didn't seem much of a choice. 'Stand back over there Erin - and cover your airways. This could knock you out for a week or even kill you - I'm not entirely sure.'

With a puzzled look, Erin did as Brodie had asked and stood well back.

Brodie's stomach gurgled as he pranced stupidly in front of Ly Erg, goading him into battle. If he could get angry or scared, his powers would likely emerge. But the soldier just stood with his right hand raised demanding the heather. How could anyone be frightened of that? Brodie's stomach gurgled loudly and his bowel loosened. He needed to make sure he'd have enough so he goaded Ly Erg some more as his stomach continued to gurgle.

'I'm giving you one more chance, Brodie McHaggis. This red hand is stained with blood from my previous battles and conquests. Give me what you've got or your blood will be added to it.'

'Ok - if you say so.' Brodie's bowels went loose and flabby as he tiptoed past the feeble-looking soldier on all twenty-four of his toe-like fingers. He paused briefly, let out the smallest of puffs and then ran swiftly away from the soldier and joined Erin. They watched in anticipation as the faerie glared back at them. Ly Erg's eyes glassed over and rolled back in his head before he turned to porcelain. Cracks started to form over his body like a mosaic and he rocked slightly, back and forth. Then he keeled over onto his back where he broke up into hundreds of small fragments before fading into oblivion. All that was left was one red fragment and an outline of his body in the snow.

Erin and Brodie stared on in silence. Erin eventually found some words.

'Wow Brodie - what was in that?' She kept her scarf pulled tightly around her face.

Brodie twitched his nose and looked puzzled. 'I've no idea. It's never done that before. We only use it against midges.'

Erin laughed. 'So if I want to avoid the sting of a Highland midge, I need take a haggis out with me! What next?'

There was movement on the patio outside the dining room. Erin pointed up the hill. 'Never mind - we've got to hurry before they all come down to the castle.' Hitching up her kilt, she clambered over the fence and Brodie sprung over it like a kangaroo before descending the steps with her towards the shore. The mist had completely cleared from the loch and they stood momentarily and watched the spellbinding display of faint green and white lights pulsating across the night sky.

Erin knelt down beside Brodie and looked into his wide, blue eyes. 'What now?'

'I'm not sure. I think maybe I'm supposed to sing.' After clearing all of his airways, Brodie nestled down beside the water and began to warble deep within his throat as each of his four nostrils fanned at different times to alter the notes. Erin reached for her camera, pressed the record button and secretly filmed him. After a few minutes Brodie stopped and scanned the loch. But there was no Nessie. Not even a ripple. Sadness filled him as his hopes faded like a summer rainbow.

Erin switched the camera to still mode and pressed the button to take a photo of Brodie. The flash startled him and he shrieked and somersaulted backwards into the water. Erin threw her head back in laughter as Brodie splashed about like a fish that had lost its fins. But she stopped laughing when something moved in the water. It was dark, but something definitely moved behind Brodie. 'Quick - get out. There's something in there. I can't see what it is - just get out!'

Brodie laughed. 'It'll only be Nessie.'

'You sure?'

He didn't question Erin or look back. He shot out of the water and cowered behind her. After everything remained calm for more than five minutes, Brodie edged out from behind Erin.

'It must've been something else. I'll need to call Nessie again, quickly,' he croaked and surveyed the flickering sky. He had to make Nessie hear him tonight. He began singing again and his enchanting, melodic tones buried Erin into a deep fantasy. She didn't see the movement in the water. Haggises never sung with their eyes open so Brodie didn't see it either as he sung, blissfully unaware of what was in front of him.

CHAPTER TWENTY

A Race Against the Northern Lights

Brodie stopped singing when he heard the sound of water dripping and he opened his eyes. Two large eyes glistened back at him. He tried getting up, but his legs had cramped and he fell into the water.

'So you've survived this place then?'

Brodie sorted himself out and looked up. A mississippi smile spread across his face. But it quickly vanished as sadness and guilt replaced it. 'Thanks for coming, Nessie. But ... what if you get caught? I can't believe you've come back for me - the stupid waste of a haggis that I am.' Another wave of guilt surged through him as he remembered Erin's lifeless body in the forest. He'd done enough damage to friends already.

'Noremac would never have forgiven me if I didn't come back for you and, well, I partly blame myself. I should've kicked your butt out of Darmaeddie Loch myself! Let bygones be bygones, we have to move quickly to get you back. The prophet in our family says there won't be another night like this for a very long time - we have to go now. It's a race against the Northern Lights. I've taken some friends with me and some net we found. Quick - you must get in it. I'll carry the net in my mouth. Whatever took you away from us two nights ago did it with some force and may try again.' Nessie sighed deeply.

Brodie looked back for Erin and panicked when he couldn't see her. 'Erin! Erin - where are you?'

Erin edged out from behind a tree.

'What are you doing up there? Quick, Nessie's here.'

Erin stepped forward hesitantly, feeling afraid of herself more than anything.

'Nessie doesn't exist. Plesiosaurs don't exist ... nor do you.

I've got to be in a cruel dream.'

Brodie marched across the pebbles and kicked Erin hard in her shin. She howled and jumped up and down as she cradled her shin.

'What did you do that for?'

'So, still think you're dreaming?'

'Thanks Brodie!'

'Will you two stop fooling around - we have to go.' Nessie's large eyes grew troubled as the patio doors in the building behind them flung open and muffled laughter filtered down the hill to the loch. Three pipers began to play the bagpipes and walked ahead of the swaying crowd as people trickled out of the doors and down the stairs toward the castle.

Brodie groaned. 'Not those dying haggises again.'

'Quick you have to go now. Those people will be at the castle any minute and you'll be spotted! Erin turned to Nessie. 'There's a bounty out on your head, Nessie. Some company has offered a reward for you and has even taken out a one million pound insurance policy in case anyone really does capture you. You must go.'

Nessie frowned and cocked her head to one side. She didn't understand Erin's babbling.

Erin pushed Brodie towards the water and pulled the net around him. 'Oh, wait!' she said pulling the net off him before running back to her rucksack. 'After all our efforts, you'll want to take this with you,' she said pulling out the wart-studded, white heather and a safety pin.

'Your own piece of very lucky white heather. I'll pin it to your rowan plait so that you don't lose it.' Erin hurriedly pierced the pin through the heather and for a split second she could have sworn she heard a faint cry. She looked about her, then shook her head and threaded the pin through the rowan plait. It had been a long two days.

'Ok - you're ready to go,' she said throwing the net back over him.

Brodie looked over Erin's shoulder at the army of peat-covered boglouts climbing over the gate and making their way down the steps towards them. Erin noticed terror fill his eyes and looked behind her.

'Quick Nessie - get him to safety.' Her warm breath curled against the cold air as she paused and gently raised her hand to Nessie's large head. Her wet skin felt warm and silky. She turned and looked down at Brodie. He was like a caged animal. A large lump formed in her throat. She'd only known him for less than two days but she knew that she'd miss the ginger-red ball of trouble-making fur.

Brodie looked back at Erin with lacklustre eyes and a knot formed in his chest. He'd miss her pale face and the warmth she provided him and realised for the first time in his life how hard it was to leave a friend. Brodie's focus returned to the giggling and sniggering boglouts as they continued to descend the steps towards them. But he certainly wouldn't miss the danger he'd encountered since he'd left home.

Quick Nessie - take me home!'

Nessie bit into the net and dragged it from the shore.

'Hurry Nessie! Hurry!' shouted Erin and turned away to kick two boglouts in the stomach and punch another one in the head. 'I'll hold them back as long as I can.'

Brodie grimaced at the sight of the boglouts snarling and spitting their peaty saliva at Erin - but she was four times their size, so she seemed to be handling them well.

'Bye Erin - thank you for everything. I'll come back and visit.'

'But you can't Brodie,' Erin reminded him.

Brodie's wide grin faded instantly as he was pulled into the water. She was right - he could never see her again. The icy water rushed past his ears as he was whisked through the loch at high speed and joined by two other plesiosaurs as they snaked hard around to the left and swam straight for the rock face. The familiar rainbow light flashed through the water and the rock face opened up. As soon as the tail of the last plesiosaur was through, the Secret of Loch Ness snapped shut.

The boglouts continued to kick and spit at Erin as she fought them off two and three at a time. But when they saw Brodie submerge into the water they simply retreated, their peaty-brown eyes staring after him in disbelief.

'We're in trouble.'

'The goblins are going to have our guts for garters.'

'We could take *her* back.'

As the boglouts argued amongst themselves, Erin looked on silently at the cold water gently lapping at the shore. She felt empty.

'Nincompoop! How do you propose we get that giant back?' The boglouts turned and stared up at Erin's tall frame. Well, she was tall to them. They waved their hands dismissively at her.

'Naaah. The goblins don't want her anyway. They wanted Gertruda back - but now she's gone forever.'

'And so are we!'

Miserable and defeated, the boglouts turned on their heels and scaled the steps muttering their discontent. As they did, they faded into thin air, but Erin could still hear their whinging voices until they too eventually faded.

She turned back to the water. It was as smooth as black glass. Tears spilled down her cheeks and she felt as though a large hand had reached into her mouth and ripped out her heart. She wiped her eyes with the back of her glove and bent down to examine the bruise on her shin from the kick that Brodie had given her. Two days ago she thought she was the most logical ten-year old in the world. Now her mind was like scrambled eggs and she'd never know what to believe in the future.

Picking up her rucksack, she threw it over her shoulder and traipsed up the steps towards the castle. After climbing over the gate, she paused briefly over the spot where Ly Erg had dissolved into the snow and picked up the one small fragment of red hand that remained. She watched silently as all footprints from Ly Erg and the boglouts slowly dissolved into the snow until there was no evidence of any mythical creatures having ever been there. Erin was totally unaware that she was being watched by a dark, cloaked figure from the shadows of the night.

CHAPTER TWENTY-ONE

Hoodwinked

Although Brodie felt a deep sadness to be leaving Erin, he couldn't help but feel immense relief and pleasure to be finally going home. The loud snoring from the haggis community was a welcoming sound as he bolted down the snowy hillside into Drumdrui. But, not surprisingly, there was no snoring coming from the McHaggis burrow.

A pang of fear sliced through his stomach as he prepared himself. He'd been through worse things than he could ever imagine would happen to him and survived them, but he was still frightened of having upset his parents. At least he was beginning to get used to the thought of having to eat a centipede or two.

As he thought over his story about being attacked by the kelpie - although his father probably wouldn't believe it, but it had to be more believable than everything else that had happened - he smiled proudly at the heather hanging from his ankle. He had set out to find the truth behind the myths and he had done more than that. He had rid the haggis of its darkest enemies and they could now live in less fear with the discovery of the real Silent Protector. He wondered how he could persuade the others what it was.

*

Erin nervously made her way to the castle and paused at the archway as she surveyed its thick, stone walls. The floodlights shone brightly on the castle ruins, and well-dressed celebrities buzzed around the undulating grounds as they looked at everything they could and took photos of even more. Erin's father sidled up to her smiling widely.

'Where did you get to?'

'Oh, nowhere really.'

'You know,' he said thoughtfully. 'I think your mother's going mad. First she thought she heard the piper practicing over here, but he hadn't even left the dining room.'

Erin shut her eyes slowly as she realised her mother must have heard Brodie.

'Then, she claims to have just seen Nessie swimming past the castle. Now, what would you say to that?' said Ralph smiling encouragingly.

Erin stayed calm and tried to muster a smile to cover her shock about what her mother had seen and heard. 'I'd have to say that Mum has been drinking too much champagne. You know there's no such thing Dad.' Once upon a time Erin would have strongly believed that.

'Exactly what I thought you'd say - and I agree with you,' said Ralph grinning boyishly as he circled his arm around his daughter. 'Where is your coat? You're freezing.'

Erin lowered her eyes to the ground and remained silent whilst Ralph took off his black, woollen coat and wrapped it around his shivering daughter. She looked up at her father and smiled gratefully as they stood in a pleasant silence watching the guests.

Brenda rushed across to them with her mobile phone at her ear, looking rather stressed. 'Now Rose, let's not jump to conclusions. Yes Rose. But … yes … no … look, we have to discuss this rationally.' Brenda removed the phone from her ear and frowned at it, her lips slightly trembling. 'She hung up on me. Can you believe that?'

'What's Rose Stewart doing phoning you tonight - of all nights?' asked Ralph curiously.

'Well … it's just so strange.'

'What's so strange, Mum?'

Brenda looked distant for a few moments before she shook her head sharply and responded. 'Our house alarm was going off. So Rose and Owen went across to see what the trouble was. They thought we had burglars. They opened the door and deactivated the alarm and took a look around the house. No doors were forced open, no windows were broken. They switched the light on and …'

'And what?' asked Ralph.

'Well … Rusty was just sitting on our kitchen floor staring at them. He ran towards them and greeted them.'

'Well, that's a first,' said Erin sarcastically. 'Normally he'd be barking at them too.'

'Well, yes - he's a completely different dog now apparently. It's definitely Rusty, but he's just so … friendly. But, Rose is accusing us of kidnapping him. How on earth did he get in our house?'

Ralph scratched his head as he thought about that one. 'Why would we leave a dog in the house and put the alarm on - it just doesn't make sense. Owen will see sense. Erin - you've got photos of those strange paw prints. We've still got that animal sample back at home and the heather. It'll be ok - nothing to worry about.'

'Yes - I told Rose that too. We have to sort this out when we get home.'

Erin lowered her eyes to the ground. She had destroyed the photos and the rubbish had been collected that morning. Her stomach then dropped like a stone as the true force of reality hit her. She had left the white heather on the kitchen windowsill. The spell that Brodie had cast on Rusty obviously wasn't permanent. It had lasted only twenty-four hours. Rusty had come back, but as a friend not an enemy. She looked across the castle wall out to the blackness of the loch as she realised what danger Brodie had taken with him to Dunroamin. But would the spell be able to turn Gertruda into a friend? Cold shivers ran through her body as she realised that Gertruda had hoodwinked them.

Gertruda had known that Noremac would never kill anything so she knew that the heather would only be a temporary measure. Of course, a piece of heather lying around the hillside would never seem strange to a haggis, but a stunned enemy lying in front of them would. Clever. But outwitted by Gertruda. She had deliberately goaded Brodie into taking her from the forest - invited out by non-faeries - taken out by Erin in her rucksack. But would Gertruda emerge as a friend or foe? Large tears welled in her eyes as she remembered Ly Erg's threat to Brodie - he maybe hadn't been such a feeble soldier after all.

The floodlights went out and only the castle tower remained dimly lit by the torches of fire carried by the waiters. Everybody gazed upwards and admired the Northern Lights across the clear, Highland sky, lost in their own imagination - except for Erin. The sound of Dion Cameron's voice added to the mystical evening as she sang Auld Lang Syne. Erin's blood curdled when she focused on the piece of moss-speckled heather that was pinned to her dress. Somehow, she had to warn Brodie.

*

A rustle of leaves echoed around the tops of the rowan trees and interrupted Brodie's pleasant thoughts. He craned his neck upwards and suddenly realised that there were no leaves on the trees and there was no wind. He recalled the dryad's words about only revealing themselves when they were needed - when there was danger. Brodie's eyes grew troubled and the smile vanished instantly from his face as he looked down at the heather. What had he done?